No Panic

Robin Gilford

iii

Alison.

With best wishes.

Robin Gilford.

Dec. 2021

Acknowledgements

My grateful thanks go to Ian and Sue for all their help.

Preface Book Two

When the parents of Simon and Vanessa fail to return from holidaying in Cornwall, investigations begin. It's a long hot scorching summer, and the West Country is even busier than usual with extra visitors. But when two persons mysteriously disappear without trace, no one is prepared for the dark secrets that are uncovered. Police officers Freeman and Soloman start to unravel the case amidst great changes in their own personal lives.

Revised Edition

This trilogy was written before the Coronavirus pandemic struck in 2020. Social distancing and the wearing of masks were not an issue.

This trilogy is best read in order

No Trace

No Panic

No Fear

Chapter 1

'Blackbird, blackbird,' he quietly gasped, as Sonia twisted the rope one last time.

There was evidence of sexual activity where he lay naked and motionless on the bed. Sonia checked his pulse but his lifeless body lay limp and inert. Around his ankles and wrists, four separate pieces of rope tied him to the corners of the large antique oak bed frame. A fifth piece was tied around his neck and it was here that Sonia stood, gazing intently at the open eyes that were staring back at her. She moved away quickly to the window. The room was stuffy and warm but once the window had been opened, a cooling breeze entered from the summer night air outside. As one breath inside had left, another had replaced it from outside. All was quiet as Sonia moved back to the bed and deftly passed her hand over the eyes of the corpse in front of her, closing them both in one swift movement. He had been a good looking man just turned forty.

'Green, green,' she gasped in the next room.

It came out almost as a stutter but for her also, they were her last words as Trevor tightened the rope around her neck. She lay naked and face up on the low bed frame, one last twitch as life eased away from her. Here too there were signs of sexual activity. She had been an attractive woman in her early forties but Trevor had ended that.

1

She too was tied to the four bed corners. The rope cut tightly into her wrists and ankles and again, similar to the next room, a rope had been tied around her neck. Unlike the man next door, a rough hessian bag had been placed over her head. Trevor walked around the bed and opened the window. More cool night air entered the stone cottage.

In the room next door, Sonia had untied the ropes and was beginning to loosen the white sheets that the man lay upon. Having slackened them all, she entered the back bedroom, where Trevor stood gazing down at his lifeless victim. She beckoned him and he followed her silently into the front bedroom. The two bedside lights now provided an eerie glow, where once they had created a warming atmosphere. The curtains swished gently in the breeze created by the open window behind. It was two o'clock but neither Sonia nor Trevor showed any signs of tiredness, as they moved about their tasks, in an automated fashion.

The   safe   words   had   not   been   safe   at   all.

Chapter 2

The street outside was empty, except for a few late night revellers staggering home from the town's two night clubs, which had just closed. The low voltage street lamps provided a warming glow, not that any warming was needed, for despite the hour the temperature remained at twenty degrees. A warm breeze wafted in from the seafront, two streets away. This was Looe on a Friday night turning into Saturday morning. It was June and the weather was especially good, promising the continuation of a long hot summer. There was an upbeat, positive feel to the small seaside town. The weather was just what the holiday makers and residents wanted. The days were long and filled with warmth and sunshine. The bars and pretty harbour side restaurants were busy, full of happy people eager to spend their money. The beach was of golden sand, clean and sheltered, an ideal holiday destination for all and soon children would be adding to the busy throng, once they had broken up from school. Fishing and day boats bobbed gently in the harbour, what was there not to like? All seemed good, a very far cry from what was occurring at that very moment in Treworthy Cottage.

How could such a grizzly scene be unfolding in such an attractive and tranquil place?

There was good and evil either side of that front door. The two sides were unrealistic, horrendous and drastic. On one side, warmth and happiness, on the other darkness and evil. Incomparable in its awfulness, how would this situation resolve itself?

Outside the last of the club revellers wound their way up the hill, past the deathly cottage, unaware of what was happening behind the pretty front door.

A little later the street became completely empty. On both sides there were parked cars. It was almost a desolate scene, except for a ginger tom cat, which slid under a low sports car. He crossed over the road, passed under another car, and walked a short way along the pavement, before jumping onto a low wall and dropping down the other side through a tall and thick hedge. It was his usual route.

At the bottom end of Harbour Street, aptly named because it started at the harbour, were small gift shops on either side but further up as it gently climbed, these gave way to a mixture of houses. There was a row of terraced properties with small front gardens. Many of these had been turned into holiday cottages but not all.

Further up the street, the houses became much larger with substantial front gardens and drives. One had been converted into an art gallery. It was a successful business and as such could accommodate art and sculptures on both floors.

At the top of the road, there was a theatre, which was popular with both tourists and locals. At Christmas, there was the usual pantomime with its regular following.

A gentle breeze was now blowing off the sea and a loose poster on the notice board outside tore free from its drawing pin mountings.

Two streets away, on the seafront, a young couple emerged from behind a sea defence. Having rearranged his clothes, he held out his hand for the girl, whom he helped up. They kissed and embraced briefly and walked off arm in arm along the promenade. The night was still young for them. They were full of life and vitality.

Down on the quayside, some fish and chip papers idly fell out of a bin and scampered up the street in the breeze.

At five am, movement started in the small town as it began to come to life for another sunny and busy day.

Mr Brooker left his cottage in Harbour Street and made his way to his little bakery at the back of the Castle Hotel. He had a thriving business supplying the hotel and his little shop. It was now light as he made his way along the pavement.

Not bad for a Friday night, he mused, realising that he had not been disturbed by noisy revellers outside during the night especially as it had been a Friday. He quite often went to bed even earlier in order to cope with the extra demand for his cakes and breads the following day.

Another hot one, he thought. Even at this time of day, he could sense it.

All in all, Looe was a charming place to live. A committed community, a sheltered spot on the south coast of Cornwall, a golden beach, restaurants, bars, a theatre and an art gallery all made for a popular destination.

Chapter 3

'Bing bong,' the sound came over the aircraft sound system and the announcement was made that the aircraft would soon be landing at Bristol.

Nigel Rathbone hated flying, especially the take off and the landing. He found no joy in either experience. He and his wife Susan were returning from a long overdue holiday.

'Pass me a sweet,' he said.

She passed the bag to him. It was nearly empty now.

'We will be down in a few moments, love,' she said grasping his hand. 'It was a lovely holiday wasn't it?'

The plane was beginning to descend and Nigel had closed his eyes.

Close and long term friends had let them have the use of their villa, set in the north east of Lanzarote, down a bumpy track. The remoteness had done them both the world of good, no noise at all, just peace and quiet, spectacular views, sunshine and warmth. The two terraces had provided ideal spots for secluded sunbathing and barbequing.

The two weeks had passed in a rested haze. The weather had been hot. At midday it had been a little too warm and they had spent those hours in the shade of a wide veranda covered in orange bougainvillea. First thing in the morning, they had flung open the French doors onto one of the terraces and Nigel had stood everyday looking at the sea. It had glinted like a thousand jewels as the sun continued to rise into the sky passing overhead until eventually dropping in the west like a big orange ball.

It had been like a fabulous dream for them both, after the stresses and strains of the renovations of Treworthy Cottage and at the same time, developing and building up their art gallery business.

Blue skies and a deep blue, sometimes turquoise sea churned on the rocks, a mile away and down on the shore. Edged in white frothiness where it met the sea, they had watched from afar. Sometimes it gently lapped and at others it pounded with such force that it was surprising that the black lava rocks did not crack or break.

On this island, along with the other Canary Isles, the sea fell away into such great depths that it had enormous power at the shoreline. But this little island, like the others, stood up to the constant ravages of the sea, with little erosion, providing a wonderful, colourful and varied seascape. At other times the blue water was flung into the air and landed with a great force.

They were back on the ground now, sixteen hundred miles away from their idyllic paradise and as the aircraft doors were opened, they were at least greeted by the extra warmth of that June Sunday evening. It may have been mid-summer and wet but the South of England was experiencing something of a heatwave. On this evening the rain added a tropical element. It poured down as they hastily made for the terminal building. As they raced inside towards passport control, they reached for their papers.

After the routine monotony of passing through the airport and collecting their car, they at last made their way down the motorway towards Devon. At Exeter they proceeded onto the main road. It seemed a long and endless journey after an early start and a four hour flight.

'Just as well we have Maria opening up for us tomorrow. I really don't think I shall be in much of a fit state first thing,' Nigel said, breaking the silence to his wife.

Eventually at one thirty on the Monday morning they arrived back at Tinterdale House, their home in Harbour Street. They unpacked their few bags and fell into bed, weary from their travels.

Chapter 4

Simon Tamworth woke with a start. He felt tired but as it was daylight, he turned his head to pick up his mobile. It was seven thirty, which was his usual time for waking and getting up. Today, as with the last few days, he had no inclination whatsoever. He felt drained and exhausted. For the last few nights he had hardly slept at all and on this particular Tuesday, he had lain awake for what seemed the whole night, only falling into a deep sleep at five am when the birds were in full dawn chorus and it was light.

He tossed aside the sheet, swung his legs out of bed and made for the door. As he crossed the landing on his way to the bathroom, he stopped outside his sister's door and knocked.

He gently called, 'Vee, it's just passed seven thirty, are you awake?' He waited patiently for the affirmative voice and continued, 'I'm having a shower now and then I think I had better make that call. Do we need to discuss the situation anymore?'

Simon was nineteen and mature beyond his years. All his life he had had to look after his sister Vanessa who was four years his junior. Their parents had often gone away at weekends. To begin with, they had been left with an aunt, on their father's side of the family. As Simon had grown older, these duties had fallen to him and as such he and his sister were very close and supportive of one another. She was very fond of her brother and realised how much she depended on him.

Better be a cold one, Simon thought as he turned on the shower. I need to be awake, despite the lack of sleep.

Five minutes later, as he retraced his steps back across the landing, Vanessa's door opened and a sleepy eyed figure appeared from the darkness of her room. She was not fazed at seeing her brother's naked body on the landing. He never seemed to wear any clothes at home. The cold water drops glistened on his body for he wasn't one for using a towel.

'What time are you off?' She asked croakily.

'In about half an hour but I must make that call. I am so worried about Mum and Dad.'

He returned to his bedroom, retrieved his shorts and vest that were his regulation uniform, for his job as a lifeguard at the local swimming baths in Chichester. It was already far too warm for him to even consider the necessity of his matching regulation hoodie top. Glancing quickly in the mirror, he straightened his short dark hair with the help of his fingers and he was ready to prepare their breakfasts.

Simon and Vanessa had only lived in this house for two months. It was a brand new four bedroom executive-style property on a new estate. It was all that their mother, Bridget, had ever wanted and they had only been able to afford it after the sudden and unexpected death of her sister in law. Very sadly she had passed away after contracting a rare form of stomach cancer. Having no children or husband, Anna Tamworth had named her brother as the sole recipient of her estate. The loss of his very close and dear sister had taken its toll on Chris. After the initial shock and spurred on by his wife, they had managed to purchase their new dream house and at the same time keep their old terraced home in a quiet back street nearby.

Simon had become accustomed to where everything had been placed. Vanessa, however, was more dreamlike and constantly asked her brother where she could find the items needed to fulfil her day to day life. She would help if asked, but why bother if you had a wonderful brother?

10

Simon emptied some muesli into a bowl and placed a cup to receive coffee from the Gaggia machine. It had been at their father's insistence that they had this costly gadget. It had been paid for with the last of the legacy. Since its arrival in the household it had grown to be very popular with everyone.

Without further ado, Simon dialled one zero one, the non-emergency police number. He and Vanessa had decided that it was an emergency but not critical, in its immediacy. He and his sister had already discussed what needed to be said and how it would be conveyed. They had spoken about this at length over the previous evenings when it had become apparent that something was not altogether how it should be, so he felt confident that he should proceed.

Simon's call was answered almost immediately, with that cool calm efficiency. Simon could hear that the female operator was in some kind of control room, as there were many other conversations going on around her.

'I would like to report that our parents are missing,' he started.

'What is your name, sir?'

'Simon Tamworth.'

'And the names of your parents?'

'Chris and Bridget Tamworth.'

'And when did you last see them and at what point did you feel that they were missing?'

'They left a week ago last Saturday and should have been back last Saturday. I can get no answer from them. They went on holiday to Liskeard in Cornwall, to a holiday cottage. I have rung the agency and they say that as far as they were concerned, everything was in order, as the cottage was spotlessly clean and none of their belongings had been left behind.'

As he uttered these sentences, suddenly the enormity of what he was saying hit him. This was real now. There was no turning back.

'When did you make that call and to what number?'

'Yesterday, Monday.'

'What is the name of the letting agency, their address and telephone number?'

Simon had these to hand and read out the relevant details.

Throughout the conversation, Simon had heard consistent typing at the other end of the phone line. He felt as if he was on a production line. He was being taken seriously, very seriously but it was all rather matter of fact. These may have only been facts to the person he was speaking to but to him and his sister, it was real. Their parents were missing, seemingly without trace.

The operator repeated back what Simon had told her to make sure that the details were completely accurate. She then gave him an incident number, 'A senior officer will call you to take this further. What is the best number?'

'My work number, it's the local fitness centre.' He called out the number. 'I'm a lifeguard in the swimming pool. Whoever calls will need to be put through to me.'

'If you think of anything else, or want to call again, please use the incident number as a reference point and all that you have told me will be available to the next operator.'

'Thank you,' and with that the hardest phone call of his life was finished.

Simon put his mobile on the breakfast table and started to eat his muesli. He had ten minutes before he needed to leave the house.

It would all be fine he thought, as he drank his coffee. The police now know the whole situation. There is nothing more I can do.

Vanessa appeared in the doorway and placed her cup in the Gaggia machine. She still looked just as sleepy.

'How did it go?' she asked.

'They just took some details and told me that another officer would call me later, so I have given them the swimming pool number. You okay for school today? Better tell the head what is going on.'

'I'll see how it goes,' Vanessa replied, not committing herself.

'Are you okay for time?' he continued, not wishing her to be late.

'Yes, I am getting a lift with Sharon. I told her about Mum and Dad and her mum offered to pick me up.'

'I am pleased your friend and her mum are being supportive. I am off now,' he said, draining his cup and putting on his shorts and vest. 'Remember to lock up,' he called back over his shoulder as he closed the front door.

He collected his mountain bike from the garage and pedalled off, still thinking about how his day would pan out.

Twenty minutes later, after a workout of a bicycle ride on a warm June morning, he arrived at the leisure centre. He locked his bicycle in the bike store and entered through the glass front doors. During his ride he had decided to speak first with the front reception desk and then his boss. Better be upfront with everyone about the situation, he thought.

Simon had a good working relationship with the team that he worked with. His manager, David, liked his work ethic and was hoping to keep him on, for he knew that Simon had a place at Chichester University, which would start in September.

Simon sat down at the front desk. He always got on particularly well with Karen, who liked to mother him. She had a son herself who was twenty and her maternal instinct carried on beyond her own family.

'Good morning,' he started, his usual light-hearted manner was not present, 'something I need to tell you, do you mind if we talk in the back office?'

'No problem,' Karen could tell that there was something amiss, 'what's the matter, everything alright at home?'

She opened the side door for him, 'Beverley, hold the fort, while I look after Simon, come through, what's bothering you?'

'Perhaps I had better tell Dave at the same time. It's rather important.' He stood in the doorway, unsure and unsettled, realising that he would now be repeating what he had told the police earlier. It also dawned on him that although his parents had not returned when they were expected, they were not due back to work until today, so he would have to telephone their respective places of work to explain the situation.

'Dave's not due in until ten,' Karen started realising how important it was. 'He's on a late.'

'It's like this, Mum and Dad were away last week but never returned on Saturday as they were supposed to. I've tried their mobiles constantly but neither are connecting. I did think they might be in a dead spot being down in Cornwall but I have tried them both at different times.' He sat down momentarily but stood up almost immediately and started pacing the small back office. 'I just feel that something has happened to them. They are due back at work today, so I am going to have to ring Rolls Royce at Goodwood to explain and this morning I rang the police, so I am waiting for a call from them.'

He paused, the enormity of it all was now weighing heavily on his shoulders.

'I am so very sorry,' Karen started, 'how is Vanessa?' Again, the maternal instinct came to the fore.

'She's okay, at the moment, though I don't think she has thought about the implications much. She leaves all of that to me.'

There was a flicker of a smile across Simon's face. He obviously cares very much for his sister, she thought.

She rattled on in an organised fashion, 'this morning's sessions are the usual for a Tuesday. We have the young adults with extra needs at the moment until ten and then the tiny tots with their mums or dads until eleven and then the pool is open for all. Have you got the number for Rolls Royce?'

'Yes, I am all prepared for that, thanks,' Simon answered.

'Well if there is anything else I can help with, here or out of work, please let me know. How about shopping?'

'We are fine at the moment. Mum left the freezer full.' He paused, 'I'm working with Tanya today. Please could you advise her where I am. I should have started five minutes ago.'

Karen smiled, closing the door behind her.

Simon sat and mulled it all over, for a minute or two. The current situation had started with him keeping an eye on his sister but now it was rather more than that. He was talking to the police, his colleagues at work and now he was about to call the employers of his parents.

It took several minutes for his call to be answered at Rolls Royce and there was a second wait while his call was put through to the Human Resources department. Shirley promised to let the relevant managers know why Chris and Bridget had not arrived that day. His mother worked in the public relations department, whilst his father was a master craftsman, hand- stitching leather for each individual car as they arrived in his bay. The work was exacting to say the least but very rewarding, even if some of the colour combinations for seats, head-linings, dashboards and door panels, were quite unusual. Still he had learnt to keep an open mind. His taste was more conservative and as more and more orders were from abroad, he found that tastes certainly varied greatly.

Shirley was grateful for Simon's call. Simon promised to keep her informed of progress but he left the call feeling that she was hardly interested in his predicament.

Had she really understood the implications of what he had just told her?

He left the little back office, helping himself to a paper cup of water from the chiller, deciding that he had better not shirk his duties. Besides it might help to focus his mind.

He made light of the situation with Tanya, making out that perhaps he had not fully understood what the plans of his parents had been.

Not long after, a call came through on the tannoy, 'Mr Tamworth to reception please,' it was Karen's voice.

Thinking that it was a call from the police, Simon marvelled at their efficiency but it turned out to be Dave, his boss, who as usual had come in early.

'I understand that you want a chat,' Dave started as they sat down together in his office. As soon as he saw Simon, he realised that something was wrong. His usual upbeat manner was gone. He was quiet, subdued and looking tired.

16

Simon dutifully went through it all again. This was now the fourth time in less than three hours.

'I am so sorry. If there is anything that we can do for you, just ask.' Simon knew he meant it but it didn't really alleviate how he was feeling. 'Keep me informed so that I can reorganise the rota and if you need to use this office for personal calls, you can.'

Simon was grateful for Dave's support. He left the office again feeling a little more at ease and returned to his post by the swimming pool.

'I'll be off for my break now.' Tanya's voice, from the other side of the pool, brought him back to reality. She would now be gone for forty minutes, leaving Simon to look after the pool by himself. He wasn't entirely on his own. Dave was only through a doorway and could be there in an instant. At break times, the door was always open and Dave's desk faced a window looking directly onto the pool.

I'd better focus, Simon thought to himself. I don't want to be sent home because I'm not fit for work.

It was a quiet time now anyway. Most of the mums, dads and tiny tots had left the pool as the time neared to eleven o'clock. Laughter and chat could be heard from the female changing area. Slightly less noise came from the male area. Still there were some young dads bobbing in the water with their respective little ones. Simon checked over the pool, all seemed safe.

Then at eleven o'clock, Karen's voice came over the tannoy again. 'Mr Tamworth to reception please.' Simon looked at Dave, through the window, who signalled that he was taking over. 'I think it's the police,' Karen mouthed at Simon, as he went into the back office once again.

'Good morning, is that Simon Tamworth?' It was an unfamiliar voice.

17

'Yes, who's calling?'

'I am DCI Michelle Willoughby. I am following up on your earlier one zero one call of this morning, concerning your missing parents. Can you confirm your home address please?'

Simon obliged, repeating the details again and adding, 'We are on the new estate next to the bypass.'

'You are a lifeguard at the city centre pool?'

'Yes,' Simon repeated again. He didn't seem to be adding anything new and as this was now the fifth time, he was beginning to feel frustrated. He need not have worried as DCI Willoughby broke new ground.

'My colleague and I would like to visit you at home today. When do you finish?'

'I will be home by six o'clock,' Simon responded, feeling a little more upbeat. This was at least some progress.

'We will be with you soon after six.' The call ended and Simon stood for a moment or two taking it all in.

He tried calling the mobiles of his parents again just in case there had been a terrible mistake and yet again, there was no response. He thought, is this really all happening? Can I be in some terrible dream where I will wake up at any moment? He paused for a moment, looking around the all too familiar office that he knew so well.

'Perhaps I had better pinch myself?' he said out loud.

Just at that moment, Karen appeared in the doorway, 'Are you alright?' There was kindness in her voice.

'Yes, I am fine,' Simon said rallying himself. 'This is all real isn't it? It's just that I tried Mum and Dad again, just to make sure.....that I wasn't mistaken.' There was a sombre note in his voice now and she noticed how forlorn he looked.

'And you weren't mistaken were you?' Karen said looking at him closely.

There was no need for him to answer. They both knew that this was real and that his parents were missing.

'The police are coming to the house this evening,' Simon continued trying hard to make this statement sound positive.

'Well, that's good, isn't it?' Karen responded.

'I think so, at least they are doing something. I think I had better phone Vanessa's school. I am a bit worried about her. She's got exams this time next year, so now is when she really needs to be focused.'

'Do it in your break. Tanya will be back in twenty minutes.'

Simon returned to the poolside deep in thought.

The rest of his day continued as usual. There were no poolside emergencies and he was pleased when he had spoken to the head teacher at his sister's school. Mr Woodhouse remembered Simon, as he had only left the summer before. He had been a successful head boy, well-liked by fellow students and the teaching team alike. Mr Woodhouse was very sorry and promised to keep a discreet eye on Vanessa. At the moment, she seemed to be coping.

Chapter 5

Simon's shift at the swimming baths eventually finished and he cycled home. His head was a mess. He went into the kitchen and reaching into the fridge he drank straight from the coke bottle. His mother would not be impressed, he thought. He imagined just what she would say but then she wasn't there and if she had been, he wouldn't be feeling as he did.

At precisely six thirty there was a ring on the doorbell.

'Good evening, we spoke earlier, I am DCI Willoughby and this is DS Oliver-Jones.'

'Yes, come in,' Simon said as he held the door open.

The two police officers stepped over the threshold and onto the pale lemon carpet that Simon's mother had insisted on having despite its impracticality. They stood for a moment in the large square hall, with its wide staircase rising to the side. It was still stiflingly hot and the two detectives did not look comfortable. Simon hesitated, unsure whether he should take then into the living room or the kitchen family area.

'A drink perhaps?' Simon remembered how hospitable his mother always was when there were guests in the house.

'Two glasses of water, thank you,' DCI Willoughby pronounced without any hesitation, taking the lead.

Perhaps she always worked with the other one and could speak for her, Simon thought. What was her name again?

They had moved into the spacious family room overlooking the garden and Simon noted that the two detectives were observing everything. His parents must be wealthy to afford this lovely house, DS Oliver-Jones thought.

Together they ran over the events yet again. When they had finished, the other one spoke. Simon still couldn't remember her name. 'We'd like to take a look around, if that's alright?' The last bit was added as an afterthought.

'I suppose that's alright, I'll just call my sister down, she's in her room.'

Vanessa was summoned and Willoughby and Oliver-Jones set forth to examine the house.

'What are they looking for?' Vanessa exclaimed. 'They don't think we've hidden Mum and Dad in the attic do they?'

'No, I imagine it's some routine of theirs.'

Simon had it spot on, for that was what the two officers were doing, building a picture that they could pass on.

An hour later, having looked over the whole house, double garage, shed and garden, they both appeared red faced. The heat of the day had not abated despite the fact that it was now early evening.

'We need to take any computers, iPads or laptops with us,' the DS said abruptly.

'Are you sure?' Simon said. 'What on earth do you think our parents have been up to? They both work at Rolls Royce.

This last statement was supposed to vindicate them, in Simon's naive mind. The detectives both knew better.

'We have found and taken their passports also,' DCI Willoughby continued, 'at least we know that they have not left the country.'

During this time, Vanessa had been rummaging in the fridge and had created, for herself, cheese on toast. She reached for a chilled can of Pepsi.

'Do you need me anymore?' she called into the room, as she piled her items onto a tray.

Simon looked at the detectives, who confirmed that they did not need Vanessa. She made her escape back upstairs to her room, carrying her tray, muttering something about a big school project that needed to be completed.

Willoughby and Oliver-Jones were standing by the computer. 'Are there any laptops or iPads etc that we have not found in our search or which your parents may have taken with them?' Willoughby asked.

'They took both their phones and an iPad,' Simon reported, 'they don't have a laptop or anything else.'

'Do you have a computer of any sort?' Willoughby continued with the questions.

'Just my laptop, which I use for all of my studies.'

Willoughby sighed, 'in the absence of their iPad and phones, we will just take their computer for now. It may give us some leads on their disappearance. If not, we may need to look at yours.'

They must have an idea of what they are looking for, Simon thought, or is it just a complete blank to them?

Having unplugged the necessary items, the computer was loaded into their car and Willoughby and Oliver-Jones returned to the front step.

'How is your sister taking all of this?' Oliver-Jones asked. There was never any warmth in her voice. The question seemed to have been asked not out of concern for the fifteen year old's welfare but more in case she had anything to offer the case.

'My sister is usually quiet. It's quite difficult to know what she is thinking at times but I know her well enough to feel sure that at the moment, their disappearance hasn't really sunk in. We have often been left on our own, once I was old enough to take care of her.'

'And her friends?' Oliver-Jones asked leading the questions, despite being the junior.

'She has a handful of good friends they all seem to be the quiet studious type. In fact, one of her friends has asked her mother to collect her for school in the mornings. I'm pleased, as it takes some of the concern off my shoulders.'

Willoughby decided to take charge again and changed the subject, 'We have finished here now. We will write our report and pass it over to the Devon & Cornwall Constabulary. The computer will be delivered back to you when we have finished with it and the findings will be shared with the relevant departments. You will hear from them shortly and they will keep you updated. In the meantime, we are here for you also, so if you think of anything, no matter how irrelevant it may seem, please pass it on to us or Cornwall. Here are our details.'

Contact details were handed over and then Willoughby and Oliver-Jones drove off.

It was still a very warm evening and as they left, Willoughby turned to her colleague, 'so what did you make of him and his sister and the set up there, with the parents not being around?' There was a pause before Oliver-Jones answered.

Willoughby knew exactly what she thought about it all but it was very much part of Oliver-Jones' training to be asked what she thought about it post interview and for them then to have a discussion. This all had to be done in conjunction with compiling their report, which needed to be emailed as soon as possible to the Devon and Cornwall constabulary.

Willoughby and Oliver-Jones had been working together for two years. They had a good working relationship and had learnt each other's strengths and weaknesses. Although she held the more senior rank of Detective Inspector, Willoughby was younger than her colleague, who had joined the force later in her life. There wasn't anything that they could not handle but Willoughby had learnt a long time ago that taking a hard line was not the answer on every occasion. Yes, there were instances where it was appropriate but one had to be able to analyse each case individually. This particular case required a more sensitive nature, certainly with Simon and Vanessa and experience gave her a good idea to the family set up. Michelle Willoughby was happily married, though at times she hardly saw Mike. They had no children and Willoughby had given her career all the dedication that it needed.

Justine Oliver-Jones had had a previous career in the army. She had a ten year old son, Andy, from a previous relationship but now was happily married to Linda, who was a stay-at-home mum. They also had two foster children and as a result it was a busy household. Their home was not a quiet one and when Justine had a difficult case, she often spent extra time at work.

'They are obviously used to being on their own,' Oliver-Jones started, 'and looking after themselves. It's hard to understand why the parents leave them and we are not sure how often this happens. My guess is quite often. The son looks after his sister well and the house is clean and tidy. It's not the average household with teenage youngsters and absent parents. Getting the IT department to analyse the computer will be helpful and hopefully revealing.'

'We can put all that in the report,' Willoughby summarized, 'I agree with you, that is a good start.'

They arrived back at the station and started work on the all-important report. The computer was unloaded and handed over to the IT department.

Back at the house, Simon was considering what to do next. He felt restless and ill at ease. He hadn't found much comfort in the police interview. He had not warmed to either of them despite their offers of support. Now, he felt isolated. It had all been so matter of fact. What was he supposed to do now?

He decided to clear his head and go for a run. He liked to keep up a regular exercise routine and often went out having discovered a variety of good off-road routes from their home on the edge of the countryside. 'Just off for a run, be back in half an hour,' he called up the stairs to Vanessa.

He left a note on the breakfast table as she probably had headphones on and would not want to be disturbed. Despite it being nearly eight o'clock, it was still warm. There was no breeze and it was humid and muggy. He didn't bother with a vest or T-shirt and set off left out of the front door. The properties in this road were finished and occupied with new residents. At the end he turned left again on to a boundary road. Beyond this were open fields. He was a fit man and the humidity and heat made no difference to his ample capabilities. He ran on, big strides from his long legs, landing gently on his toes like a big cat, as his running instructor had advised.

The houses here were unfinished, like big skeletons. Piles of earth with broken water pipes and bricks lay abandoned in front where in future there would be green lawns and flower beds.

Now as he ran on, he was surrounded by concrete foundations in the making and then as he rounded another bend, he was free, running down the old footpath, with a green field to his right and a wood in front of him. He sprinted along, with rivulets of sweat running down his brown torso. Soon after entering the wood he stopped. This wasn't part of his fitness regime, it was a time to be away from everyone else, to give himself a mental rest from the uncertainties of his current situation.

He soon recovered his breath and looked around. The trees were small in this part, chestnuts and beech and their vibrant green leaves gave the wood a verdant feel. Underfoot the ground was mossy with patches of lush grass here and there. He slipped out of his running sandals and put his feet on the cooling ground. Wriggling his toes was a relaxing sensation, as the blades of grass moved between them. He sat down on this luxurious floor covering and lay back, the cooling moss providing welcome relief to the sweat on his back. He closed his eyes and cleared his mind of all his troubles. Overhead, a bird sang. The cheerful chirping broke the silence. He closed his eyes again and took a deep breath. He held it in for a full ten seconds and then let it all go. This was repeated ten times and by the end of this relaxation technique, Simon felt mentally calmer. He lay there for a few moments, the warmth of the air and the stillness all around washed over him, in a wave of comforting reassurance. After some time, he came to and sat up.

How long had he been lying there? He wasn't sure. It was still light but he knew he had to return home and so springing to his feet and picking up his sandals, he ran barefoot back to the road. He would have continued on in this manner but the road surface was cracked and uneven, with lumps of tarmac here and there. He bent down and having fastened his sandals he sprinted home.

He came in through the front door and as there was no sign of Vanessa, he went upstairs and gently knocked on his sister's bedroom door.

'You okay,' he called softly. 'I'm back now, just making something to eat. You want anything?'

'No thanks, I'm fine,' the equally soft response came back.

At that moment Simon heard his phone ringing. As he picked it up from the bedside table a few paces away in his room, he saw that it was his work colleague, Karen.

'Hello Simon, sorry to intrude, just ringing to see how you are? How did you get on with the police? They have left, haven't they? Just wanted to make sure you are alright.'

'Yes fine, they left about an hour and a half ago. Just got in from a run,' he used the term loosely.

'Have you eaten?' the questions flowed.

'Just about to.'

'As long as you are alright, I'll see you in the morning.'

'Yes, see you in the morning, early night I think.'

After the briefest of showers, he returned back downstairs to the kitchen, where he made a sandwich from the ham and cheese that remained in the fridge. He entered the lounge and turned on the television to watch the news. The room seemed so large not helped by the empty sofa and chairs. During the short time that they had lived in this house, his parents had always sat on them at this time of day. The room was devoid of their happy voices and the sound from the television did little to fill the gap. Half an hour later, having eaten the sandwich he returned to his bedroom, lay on the bed and sleep soon descended.

Back at the police station, Willoughby and Oliver-Jones were still compiling their report but by ten o'clock they had finished and it was sent through to the police headquarters at Bodmin.

Chapter 6

Detective Constable Ore Soloman gradually came to and opened his eyes. It was eight am. This was a much later waking time for him than customary. Above his bed was a large south facing roof window. Brightness flooded in and down on him. He had slept well. This morning he hadn't been woken by his alarm and most unusually, he had a day off. In fact, he had the rest of the week as holiday and it was now only Wednesday. Days off were a rarity and he was going to enjoy this period away from the stresses and strains of police detective work. Apart from the odd day here and there and a short period at Christmas, this was his first real holiday since he had arrived in the South West from Reading, just over a year ago. His boss, DCI Gavin Freeman had strongly suggested that he took some well overdue leave. As he lay in the sunshine, he stretched down the bed and luxuriated in this thought.

It was to be a time of double happiness as it was the first occasion that his lover had managed to have some time off work, again for a few days. The expectations between the two of them were high and justifiably so. Five whole days, before they were expected back on duty in their respective careers, to rest, recuperate and more importantly get to know each other.

The heat from the sun was already warm. It had been a hot night in more ways than one and Ore had found that the unaccustomed heat from another body in his bed had been rather overwhelming. It had been a wonderful new experience. He gazed at the clear blue sky, through the roof window. Most mornings he did this, almost as if in prayer.

It was so warm that he had pushed the light duvet off himself during the night and this had formed a ridge down the centre of the bed. Richard had done the same thing.

He sprung lightly to his feet and made his way round to the other side of the bed. He bent down to lightly kiss the forehead below, whispering, 'Good morning, I hope you slept well. Would you like a cup of tea or coffee?'

Richard moved his arm and his hand lightly brushed Ore's thigh. 'A tea would be wonderful. It's a long time since anyone brought me tea in bed. I slept very well, eventually, thank you,' he purred.

Ore paused for a moment, gazing down at the perfect body before him. Well it was perfect in his eyes. Tanned and only lightly muscled, there was just a hint of the beginning of some tummy fat. At least, he's not that vain and self-absorbed, Ore thought.

He made his way to the kitchen. It was only a one bedroom flat, on the top floor, the second. But the four rooms, bedroom, bathroom, lounge and kitchen area were all of reasonable size. It suited Ore very well and was convenient for his work, a short walk away from the police headquarters on the outskirts of Bodmin.

He filled the kettle and pushed the switch to boil. Placing two mugs and the teapot close by, his thoughts wondered again. His life had greatly changed since that meeting at the end of October when he had first met Richard. He hadn't thought anymore of it, being professional and on duty at the time. He had obviously made a big impact on him. This had led to Richard calling him when he was at his mother's fiftieth birthday celebrations. In all innocence he had gone to Richard's home in Clifton, Bristol, believing he was on police business, when in fact Richard had quite a different agenda. Here they were now, both physically and mentally. What a long way he himself had travelled down his own path. He had visited Richard a few times on those odd days off but it was quite different to be playing host in his own home. He was enjoying the new experience. A smile crept across his face and inwardly too. He felt marvellous and for the first time in his life he was happy. Nothing else seemed to matter.

He was brought back to earth by the water in the kettle coming to the boil and switching off. He made the tea and having let it brew, he took the two mugs back to the bedroom, fully intending to climb back into bed, but just as he placed one mug next to Richard, he heard his mobile ringing in the lounge.

Police training took over. That ring tone belonged to Freeman and sure enough as he picked it up, he read the word, Boss.

What could he want? Ore thought. It was he who had encouraged him to take this leave.

'I'm really sorry, something's come up. You know that I wouldn't ask unless really necessary but apart from that I think this could be really

30

beneficial to you. Have you got anything on today? Could you come in?'

Ore felt the bottom drop out of his world. It was as if the air had very slowly been released from an enormous balloon, which had previously been filled with happiness and lovely thoughts. Now they were showering down around him very slowly, only to die as they touched the ground.

How dare he use the beneficial card as a means of bribing him to come in when he so needed and deserved this break? Was he really worth so little to his boss and couldn't he use the help of someone else? Sometimes, his thoughts flowed, there were more important things in life than a career. Why was life so unfair? It wasn't as if he asked for much.

'Are you still there?' Freeman's voice came again.

'It's a bit awkward, really,' Ore was struggling with his predicament. Just what was so urgent on his first morning off? Thinking quickly, he replied, 'I'm a bit busy at the moment, I'll call you back in ten minutes.'

As he finished the call, he looked across at Richard, who had pulled a very unhappy face and was mimicking wiping tears.

'Please don't tell me your boss wants you in today,' he said, patting the sheet where Ore would lie, in a come back to bed gesture.

'I'm afraid he does, the bastard,' Ore replied, 'and I am going to have to go in, at least for part of today, to see what's so urgent.' He emphasised defiantly.

He rang Freeman back and said that he would be there in about half an hour.

'That's such a shame, after all our plans for today, so perhaps the quicker you are gone, the quicker you will be back.'

31

Ore made no further comment, as deep down he thought that it would be unlikely but there was always hope.

Ten minutes later, Ore was out of the shower, dressed in his usual black jeans and long sleeved T-shirt and was hurriedly eating a bowl of muesli.

'Help yourself to anything, take your time, have a wander around Bodmin's exotic range of shops and coffee bars and I'll message you with my progress. There's a key on the side for you.'

With that, he was out of the door and after his fifteen minute walk he was knocking on Freeman's office door.

Chapter 7

Richard Edwards was thirty six and general manager at a large five star hotel in the centre of Bristol. It was a prestigious role which came with many responsibilities but he had worked long and hard to reach this position and it was well deserved. He had worked his way up from the bottom when he had started at sixteen as a porter. After many years of working hard, attending night school and day release classes he had achieved a degree in hotel management. As a result of all his experience, there weren't many situations that he had not come across before.

There was the occasion when a group of celebrity footballers who were staying had insisted that the swimming pool and jacuzzi be reopened after its normal eleven pm closure, solely for their benefit. The hotel security team had been involved at two am and several of the footballers had to be taken to hospital after several had slipped on the pool side. The following day the pool had had to be closed for deep cleaning after the previous night's shenanigans. Thankfully the hotel had it in their terms and conditions that damages would be charged for and the hotel had benefited financially from a large settlement from the football club.

Even the local paper and radio station had been involved with a lengthy article and news feature about the deplorable behaviour of the visiting team. This had put the hotel under a spotlight and helped with its publicity.

It was a popular establishment and did well under Richard's management. As a result, he was well thought of within the hotel chain and by the chief executive officer.

Richard was a fit man. He needed to be to run this big enterprise. Most mornings, he did a short workout in the hotel gym. He did this incognito alongside guests and Bristol's fitness fanatics, who came into the hotel from their outside lives. The spa staff were under strict instructions not to communicate or acknowledge him more than a cursory good morning or afternoon. This way he was able to overhear guests' conversations and possible comments about the hotel.

Afterwards he would slip away through the main foyer, taking the sweeping stairs to the first floor, passing through a door marked 'private' at the top into his office. At the rear of this was a small bedroom and bathroom, for his personal use. Here he could shower and dress at his leisure, over breakfast, whilst he prepared for the day ahead.

Right from the start of his working life he had had to work Sundays, bank holidays, evenings and for a period the night shift. Even now, he had not forgotten those times, as he took his turn dovetailing around the others in the senior management team. He didn't have to work like this. It was his choice, a way of keeping his hand in at grass roots level and he was respected for it. Very often he learnt how his team were feeling about issues that had arisen during the normal course of events and was able to address these immediately.

During his working life, he had met many members of staff who were passing through. He had had several personal offers and some of these he had taken but nobody had remained. Meanwhile he had managed to buy a house in Clifton, a smart suburb of Bristol. He had had the property renovated to a high standard and his own taste. If he had chosen to be further out of the city, he could have afforded something much larger but convenience was one of his priorities. Being relatively close to the centre, he could walk or run to work. It was with sadness, however, that he remained alone.

Then, out of the blue, during a police investigation into the disappearance of his next door neighbour, he had fallen for the detective constable. Unfortunately, Ore Soloman had been unsure of himself having spent his adult life furthering his career. He hadn't given a second thought to his own private life. After a second meeting which Richard had instigated himself, on the pretence of wondering how the investigation was going, a positive step had been made.

Since that event, Richard had met up with Ore most weeks. Ore had travelled up to Bristol on his days off and they had got to know one another enough to know that this should continue. Richard had been looking forward to this break and was excited about exploring Cornwall. He wanted to discover the beaches and intimate coves, walk on Bodmin moor and to wander around the little town and villages.

As he lay there in the bed, he looked up at the ceiling and through the roof window, to the blue sky beyond.

Be positive, he thought, although it won't be the same I can still get up and enjoy getting out and about. I'll start with Bodmin.

An hour and a half later, Richard was sitting outside a cafe with a newspaper, sitting in the sun. Apart from a few shoppers, the street was quiet. It had been pedestrianised and as he sat there his thoughts wandered to what he knew about Ore. He knew that he had moved from his hometown of Reading, although his dark skin indicated a Caribbean heritage. Like Richard, he had an athletic frame and was five foot ten.

Ore was studying for his sergeants' exams and Richard made a mental note to support him through this and future exams too. Being that bit older, he knew what it was like to have to study. No, he decided, he wasn't going to get all uptight if Ore had to take time out to study, or even had to go into work at short notice, creating a change in their plans, as today had shown.

Ore, he decided, was lovely and worth making an effort for. Richard returned to his newspaper. The sun shone down and the temperature rose. It was good to be able to relax and concentrate on someone else. His daily thoughts usually involved his work.

At that moment, his phone rang and he was pleased to see that it was Ore.

'Glad it's you mate and not my work,' Richard got in first, 'I'm out having a coffee in the sunshine.'

'Glad to hear it, I am really sorry I can't come back, until this evening. My boss was right, it is a big one. Can't say more, you know that, bit of a rush now, got to go out, the whole team has just been briefed. Make yourself at home,' he paused, 'I am really sorry about this.'

'I understand, I'll do dinner, saw you had a slow cooker, is that okay?' Richard fired off this response, as he could tell Ore needed to go but at the same time, wanted to reassure him.

'See you later,' and with that Ore's phone went dead.

Half an hour later Richard was in the supermarket, buying the ingredients for dinner. Having returned to the flat and prepared their meal in the slow cooker, he decided to drive to Looe for an explorative visit.

Chapter 8

DCI Gavin Freeman had left his little house on the outskirts of Bodmin in a happy mood that morning. It was quite usual to have to balance a stressful job with what was often a busy home life. With a pregnant wife, who was due to give birth at any moment, and a small daughter, there was always something at home to keep him occupied. It was no use going home with a pile of work-related issues to deal with. He was expecting an easy few days, catching up on mundane paperwork. He thought that he would be able to make use of this exceptionally good weather that everyone was enjoying, by working shorter days. It would help make up for all the very long periods that he had worked, on previous cases. How wrong could he have been, for as soon as he opened his computer, there was a report marked 'very urgent', that had been sent through late the previous day, from West Sussex Constabulary, regarding two missing persons.

More missing holiday-makers, Freeman thought, jumping to a conclusion and remembering the case of 'the missing limb', which he and Soloman had investigated only the previous year. It had only been finalised a few months before.

Upon reading the report it was clear that the two missing persons had not responded to phone calls from family whilst in the later stages of their holiday. The holiday cottage where the couple had been staying would have to be investigated first.

It was just what Freeman did not need. He had called his team together and briefed them. DC Soloman had been telephoned and requested to attend and the briefing had taken longer than he had wanted. There had been much discussion about abduction, suicide and falling at the cliff edge. The long and challenging Cornish coastline had also been discussed.

'Whilst the disappearance of one person is very serious, the likelihood is that a far more serious crime has taken place if two persons go missing at the same time.' Freeman had said, summarising the briefing. 'The probability of a major incident having occurred here is much greater.' Freeman paused and a silence descended on the room, as the gravity of his words sunk in.

Afterwards, in the corridor outside the briefing room, Ore had managed a quick phone call to Richard, explaining that this was an important case and that he would be back later that evening.

'Come on,' a voice behind Soloman told him that Freeman was becoming impatient and needed him to follow him out to the car.

As they sped out of the police headquarters on the outskirts of Bodmin, further discussions took place. The sun had beaten down on Freeman's parked car and Ore felt very uncomfortable. It was not a good morning. All his plans had changed at the last minute and he had not liked leaving Richard when they had made plans to go out. Here was another big case and to top it all his boss was not in a good mood.

The police report from Sussex had included the address of the property that the missing persons had been staying at and also the address of the holiday rental company in Liskeard, which they had booked through.

Soloman and Freeman found the rental company, Blue Skies, easily enough and parked outside. They were soon sitting in the manager's office at the rear of the building.

After the formalities had taken place, DCI Freeman began, 'we are here about the possible disappearance of Chris and Bridget Tamworth, who were staying in one of your properties in Liskeard last week. What can you tell us about this matter?'

Zara Oakley, the manager, was slightly taken aback by the abruptness of this approach. She was more used to smiling at people, even when she didn't want to, and making them feel good about their forthcoming holiday. She was however a professional and so with a slight smile to ingratiate herself with the policeman, she turned to her computer, as if all the answers lay hidden within.

'I'll just check,' she started, 'let's have a look. The Tamworths had booked The Old Smithy in Liskeard.' Peering further into the screen, 'they left as the booking says, last Saturday. Yes, that's right a week booking, Saturday to Saturday.' Freeman was just about to make a comment but Ms Oakley was on a roll, 'I'll just confirm the check-out notes from the cleaning company, see if there is anything untoward there.' After a few brief seconds, she continued, 'no, all seems in order, key placed in the key safe and all was clean and tidy. Nothing broken or left behind. Model guests I think, apparently they left a card saying that they had had a good time and had enjoyed the cottage. We always make a note of when the cleaners entered, just in case the guests are very slow to pack up. Some are, whilst others leave as early as possible to beat the holiday traffic,' she finally stopped for breath and there was a pause.

'You are quite sure they left on Saturday?' Soloman began.

'They were not in when the cleaners arrived and there was no sign of suitcases or clothes so I assume that they had gone home. It's correct to assume that isn't it?' There was a hint of impatience and firmness in her voice, as if the police should dare to doubt her word. 'We are a holiday home rental agency and it is not part of our remit to keep tabs on guests. It is possible that they left earlier, I don't know.'

Soloman and Freeman were unfazed by the slight aggression in her tone.

Soloman was the next to speak, 'we will need to visit this Old ...'

'Smithy,' Ms Oakley filled in the uncertainty.

'We do need to go there now,' Freeman said with a note of urgency.

'There are new guests in. We can't have you marching in, all official like. People have paid good money and have a right to their privacy.'

'May I remind you of the seriousness of this? We have a family back in Sussex, sick with worry about their parents. We need to go straight away. We can't have any more delays or hold ups in this investigation and we will need keys.'

Zara Oakley tapped away and found the postcode and then reaching down under her desk she retrieved the relevant property keys from the safe.

Gathering up her handbag and rising to her feet she spoke again, 'here are the details but on this occasion I shall come with you.' As they left the office she called over to her assistant Jane, 'just going out for a bit, manage the office for me and call the Bartholomews at The Old Smithy and ask them to return there if they are out. Assure them there is no problem with them, it's the property that we need to look at.'

Ms Oakley didn't say anymore, she knew that if it was as serious as it appeared that it might be, the fewer people who knew about the situation the better. If the press became involved, they might find that bookings faltered from the poor publicity and they could be asked many questions as if they were in some way partly to blame.

'Certainly will, Zara.' Jane nodded in agreement. She looked inquiringly at the two men and her manager, as they passed her on the way out of the building. Who were these official men who had arrived fifteen minutes ago and were now leaving with her boss to go to one of their rental properties? Her enquiring looks were not answered or fulfilled. Perhaps they are from the council, she thought. Zara Oakley hadn't looked too disturbed, so she decided that it was something or nothing. No doubt we will find out later what is going on, she thought.

She dialled the Bartholomews' number but it was not answered. She left a message on the voicemail asking them to remain in the cottage or return there as soon as possible.

Chapter 9

Ms Oakley drove the short distance to The Old Smithy with the policemen following her. It was a small Victorian terraced property with a tiny frontage. A rustic bench sat amidst some terracotta pots which were filled with colourful summer flowers, geraniums and trailing lobelia. Some small shrubs bordered the boundary wall making the space limited as a sitting area. It was a pretty place in this short terrace amongst the other properties in the street. Ms Oakley rang the bell but as there was no answer, she unlocked the door and they let themselves in.

'Wait here please,' Soloman said firmly to Ms Oakley as she looked as if she was making her way to the kitchen.

They left her in the hall and whilst Soloman proceeded upstairs rather cautiously, Freeman headed into the small and cosy sitting room at the front.

'How long did forensics say they would be?' he called upstairs.

'About thirty minutes,' Soloman replied. He had telephoned them on the way over.

'Another twenty minutes then,' Freeman said.

'What is it exactly that you are looking for?' Ms Oakley said into the air, hoping that she would get a comprehensive answer from either Freeman or Soloman.

'Routine police work, in the circumstances.' The words came back through from the open sitting room door.

It was hardly the answer that she was hoping for but she would wait for the Bartholomews to return and then hopefully find out a little more.

'Do you need me here, or shall I go and sit in the car?'

'You are free to go and wait in the car if you want to wait at all,' Freeman answered in a gentle tone. 'Can you ring the cleaners and anyone else who has been in since last Saturday? We need them here now.' A sterner tone had re-entered his voice.

'I'll go and chase up the guests.' She left the cottage and walked to her car, agitated that she wasn't being told anymore.

Fortunately, she had managed to park with a good view of the front door. She had no idea what the Bartholomews looked like as it had been Jane who had checked them in. She rang the office and asked for their number.
This time it was answered by a flustered Rita Bartholomew. 'We are on our way. We got your message but we were in a dead spot so couldn't let you know. Why do you need us back at the cottage? We were on our way to the Eden Project.'

'It's nothing for you to worry about but we do need you back here as soon as possible. All will become clear when you get back. How long will you be?'

'It's that urgent is it?' came back Mr Bartholomew's voice.

43

'Yes, I'm afraid it is but as I said, I don't think there is anything you need to worry about. How long?' Zara Oakley suddenly realised that there was just a possibility that they might know something. At that moment she hoped she had not said more than she should have. Too late now, she thought.

The afternoon was hot, continuing on as it had been for the last few weeks. Zara Oakley sat in her car with all the windows open. She was just contemplating an ice cream from the kiosk on the corner when a large unmarked panel van pulled up outside The Old Smithy. A young lady jumped out of the passenger seat and carried a large metal suitcase to the front door.

'What now?' Ms Oakley said under her breath. It's all getting very serious, she thought.

Two other cars also drove into the road at that moment and whilst it was quite a narrow street, they and the van managed to park close by. The driver of the van, a studious chap in his forties, also strode quickly back to the cottage with another case. It appeared to Ms Oakley to be heavy.

Ms Oakley recognised the occupants of the other two cars as a couple who were part of her cleaning and maintenance team. She decided that it was now time for her to go back into The Old Smithy. By the time she had reached the gate, she found that the front door had once again been closed. Must be getting a bit cramped in there, she thought. She rang the bell and was once again told to wait in the hall. The two occupants of the van were now wearing white coverall suits and everyone was wearing blue plastic shoe protectors. In the small cottage style kitchen, Freeman was interviewing the cleaner, Harriet Brown and her husband, Tommy. She had heard Harriet saying to Freeman, that there was nothing out of the ordinary inside or outside in the tiny rear garden, when they had arrived at ten am, at the start of what was a busy turnover day. She and her husband had been very pleased to find that the guests had left, the beds had been stripped and the fridge and bathroom were all spotless. It was almost too clean. They hadn't at the time, given it a second thought,

44

as it had meant that they could finish quickly and move onto the next property. 'There is nothing worse than arriving at a property, where the kitchen needs a deep clean,' she heard Harriet say. 'Tommy always starts in there.'

Meanwhile DC Soloman had been following Greg and Sue, from forensics, around the property. As they came down the steep winding staircase, Ms Oakley found herself trying to listen to two conversations.

'Well of course,' Greg was saying, 'it's much too late now. The cleaners have been in and a new set of guests have arrived. They have been in for over half a week and any clues or DNA will have been compromised. We will continue to do a thorough check and search, just in case and will have a word with the cleaner and her husband but I don't hold out much hope for any breakthroughs.'

They all squeezed into the tiny kitchen and Greg and Sue started questioning the cleaner and her handyman husband. There was nothing further that they could add.

DCI Freeman and DC Soloman emerged via the kitchen French doors into the small patio garden, 'I think we will take some DNA samples from the cleaner and her husband all the same. There isn't much more that we can check on here. Also, the guests, the Bartholomews, if they ever turn up,' Freeman said wearily, 'and ask Ms Oakley to come out here?' Soloman found her in the hall and sent her through. 'Any news on the Bartholomews?' he asked.

'They just said that they had turned around and were on their way back.'

Freeman acknowledged with a nod, 'ring your office and ask them to email through to me all the information you have on both the Tamworths and the Bartholomews, just in case there is a link. Play it down with your colleague, Jane, just say that there has been an incident and we need to do some background checks.'

45

Ms Oakley did as she was told and had just finished the call, when the Bartholomews appeared in the doorway having let themselves in. They were red-faced and looked hot and bothered. Beads of perspiration covered John's forehead.

'What is all this about and who are all these people? You've ruined our holiday.'

Ms Oakley was feeling very left out and was desperate to have her say, but before she was able to, Freeman started, 'I am DCI Freeman and this is DC Soloman.'

They both held up their warrant cards. The Bartholomews looked at each other aghast but before they could say anything, Freeman continued, 'we are investigating a possible incident that may have something to do with this holiday cottage. It concerns the previous guests.' He paused for a very brief second, 'have you stayed here before?'

'No, never and I am not sure we will come again,' answered Rita who seemed the more upset of the two.

'Was there anything remotely odd about the cottage when you arrived? I believe that was about two pm on Saturday last.'

'No, everything was how we were led to believe it would be. We really don't know anything.'

'Thank you for that but there are two things that will help us. Firstly, we need to take DNA samples from you for exclusion purposes and secondly we will put you in a hotel tonight whilst this property is checked by the forensic team. All your expenses will be paid. Assuming that we are happy with our findings you may be able to return tomorrow. If you would pack now and prepare to leave as soon as possible, we would appreciate it.'

Rita was not happy. 'I hate hotels and what about all the disruption to our holiday?'

Not wishing to be left out, DC Soloman interjected before anyone else could, 'we are very sorry about the disruption but it can't be helped, we are potentially dealing with a very serious crime.'

An audible intake of breath was heard at the sound of this last piece of news. Until that point, the Bartholomews had not really thought much about the implications of what was going on in this cottage, on this Wednesday in June.

'Better go and pack our bags Rit,' John Bartholomew said, shortening his wife's name endearingly.

Turning to both Greg and Sue, Freeman said, 'go with them and take their samples please.'

They dutifully obliged and followed Mr and Mrs Bartholomew upstairs.

'We are just about done here for today,' Freeman said to Ms Oakley. 'You can take them down to The Bay Tree Hotel on the corner and get them checked in.'

Greg and Sue were prepared to continue working into the night. They were a team who had a good working relationship built up over the last five years.

The cleaner and her husband were dispatched out of the door. They gave their telephone number to DC Soloman, who said that he would notify them when they could resume cleaning duties at The Old Smithy.

Ms Oakley was also about to leave, when DCI Freeman spoke again, 'you should rearrange next week's booking because I can't say at this stage if we will have finished here or not.'

Ms Oakley looked dismayed. More upheaval, she thought.

Greg and Sue returned back upstairs, where they started their investigations in earnest climbing into the loft and then moving to the larger of the two bedrooms at the front and then the smaller at the rear.

Ms Oakley collected John and Rita Bartholomew. They decided to take all of their luggage with them and she fussed around them trying to make up for their inconvenience, talking to them for all of the short journey. They arrived at the hotel, still rather disgruntled where they were checked in and advised to put everything on account. The young man on reception did his best to placate the situation with a big smile, but Rita was not happy.

'It'll be alright Rit,' John was heard to say, 'honest it will!'

'If you say so,' came back the rather abrupt reply.

Freeman and Soloman had a word with Greg and Sue, 'make sure your report is on my desk as soon as possible please.'

Greg gave a thumbs up sign, 'we will do our best, you know we will.'

Freeman and Soloman left The Old Smithy and sat in the car before moving off, 'I wasn't really expecting much, if anything at all but we have to have a starting point.' Freeman said. 'We will have a team meeting in the morning, bring us up to date in case there are any developments overnight. I'll drop you off at home and you can have the evening off. Thanks for coming in today. I know you had plans.'

'We did have plans for the rest of the week but I know this has to come first,' Soloman said a little dejectedly.

Freeman started the engine and twenty minutes later, Soloman was putting the key in his front door.

Chapter 10

Ore Soloman was greeted by the smell of a homemade stew, coming from his slow cooker. Despite the hot weather, he felt he could eat a hot meal. He had not eaten all day and although the pot contents were not ready, according to the timer, it would be good later. He lifted the lid and sniffed the contents. Someone's been busy.

He rang Richard's number.

'I'm back home, about to have a shower. Where are you mate?'

'I'm sitting in the car, will be with you shortly. I'm in Looe, so won't be too long, holiday traffic dependent.'

A short while later, there was the sound of a key in the lock and a relaxed and tanned Richard appeared in the doorway.

'So good to have you back, it has been a busy day but that didn't stop me thinking about you. I could hardly concentrate and of course the first few days of a new case are so important, not to miss anything.'

Ore smiled. It was plain to see that he was very pleased to see Richard.

'I know,' Richard said, 'I was the same, couldn't stop thinking about you either but we are back now.'

They met across the room in a big hug.

'Bought some fizz.' Richard said producing a bottle. 'It's the real stuff, I'll put it in the freezer to chill it quickly, and then we can have a drink.'

It was now five o'clock and the heat of the day carried on. The signs were that it would be a long and glorious summer evening. The shadows were relatively short and the birds were still singing. The car park belonging to the flats was busy, with people coming and going. A far cry from winter months when the weather would dictate that generally people would arrive home and immediately disappear inside.

'Shall we eat and then go out for a drink? I really like Looe and have seen a lovely beach bar today. It looks like it would attract a good crowd.'

'Sounds like a great plan,' Ore replied, 'but of course I can't drink as I have another busy day tomorrow, sorry!'

'No problem, you can drive,' Richard said, giving Ore a friendly push.

'It goes without saying, it won't be a late night. I've a feeling the next few days are going to be rather full on.'

Three hours later, Richard and Ore had blended well amongst the surfers, younger holiday makers and locals at The Sand Bar Beach Club and Cafe. It was a fabulous evening. The crowds were all in a good mood. It was warm now and the black unclouded night sky was a perfect backdrop for the bright stars. Appropriate music was playing and the drinks flowed.

Richard and Ore were very happy. It was moments like these that helped cement a relationship together.

'Shall we go for a walk?' Ore asked.

'Good idea, it's getting a bit crowded in here now.'

They set off along the beach and Ore kicked off his flip flops, wanting to feel the soft golden sand underneath his feet. The sea was a long way out, but the tide was about to turn. The beach was wide and flat. Ore felt Richard's hand looking for his and together they walked towards the water. A few others were walking on the beach and there was just a hint of light coming from the promenade. Richard picked up his sandals and together they splashed into the sea. The stresses of the day floated away and they laughed and giggled in their happiness.

As the tide came in, they wandered back off the beach and onto the promenade, eventually crossing the sea road and turning into a side street which led to Harbour Street.

There was a theatre at the top end where the roads joined. The lights were on in the foyer and the doors were open. In a short time, tonight's production would be ending and the street would be full of happy theatre patrons returning home.

'Perhaps we could go one evening,' Richard said, realising as he said it that he had no idea if Ore liked the theatre.

'I haven't been for ages,' Ore began, 'since Mum took us to a Christmas pantomime when I was about seven. It was in Reading of course. All that 'it's behind you' nonsense, I remember that I did enjoy it. We can go when I get a spare evening.'

They continued to walk down the street.

51

As they reached art gallery Richard walked towards the window. 'I'm always interested in what the locals paint,' he said peering through the glass.

The window was lit displaying large and small paintings, all by a local artist. Most were coastal scenes, but the artist was varied in his subjects. Over in the far window were some portraits and down one side these changed to cats and dogs, mostly in home and garden settings. The standard was high.

'Shame the gallery is shut, when we are passing. I think I may return in the morning. I'm assuming that I won't be fortunate enough for your company tomorrow?'

'I'm afraid not,' Ore replied, 'Boss wants us in bright and early again.'

They continued down the street past the pretty cottages. As they neared the harbour and the big hotel, The Castle, the cottages gave way to gift shops and those selling beach paraphernalia.

'I think we had better be getting back now,' Ore said, 'I need to be at my best in the morning, or else Freeman will be having words.'

They climbed back into Ore's car and set off for home and an early night.

Chapter 11

DCI Gavin Freeman was not in a good mood the following morning when he met Soloman and the rest of the team for their meeting. His wife had been rushed into hospital as it was thought that the baby was due to arrive. He had spent the night at Treliske Hospital in Truro with their daughter who naturally didn't understand why they had to leave their home and her bed where she had been tucked up asleep.

Thankfully, Gavin's mother had come to the rescue that morning. She had taken over the child minding duties and the vigil at her daughter in law's bedside.

Freeman looked a mess. He himself had decided that he was going to have a dress down Thursday and his usual impeccable style of a pristine white shirt, tie and dark suit had given way to chino trousers and a check shirt.

All in the meeting could tell that they were going to have to be mindful of Freeman's short temper and they all sat quietly and listened closely.

DCI Freeman opened the meeting, 'we have a missing couple who have been on a week's holiday staying in a rented cottage in Liskeard. The cottage was left in a near-perfect state and although we don't know when the Tamworths were last present, there is nothing to say that they didn't leave early. What we do know is that they had gone by the eleven am check out time. The forensic team have worked diligently most of the night and found nothing that they wouldn't expect to find in this sort of property. There is nothing suspicious there. So as far as The Old Smithy goes, there is nothing to indicate where the Tamworths are. Mike and Patrick are to do some door-to-door enquiries in Bury Street where The Old Smithy is located. We now have some recent photos of the missing couple, to help you and we also have an idea of some of the clothes that they may have taken with them from their son back in Chichester. They are just ordinary holiday clothes that a couple in their forties might wear. However, Mrs Tamworth apparently has a distinctive Italian red leather jacket. It is unusual both in colour and the fact that it is studded along the back seams, making it recognisable. She has that with her. Her son, Simon, remembers quite clearly it being hung up on a hanger in the car. He says it was a very expensive wedding anniversary present from his dad. This I feel is a big clue and lead. Someone might remember seeing her in it as it is definitely not a usual item of clothing for Cornwall and especially not in this heat.'

He moved swiftly on. 'We also have the make, model and registration number of their car. It is a blue Toyota Auris, brand new and apparently Chris Tamworth's pride and joy, so we are looking for that also.' He turned to George and Hilary, 'check the CCTV in Liskeard starting from Wednesday last week and look for the movements of this car. We need to know exactly where it went and what they were doing in the days leading up to their disappearance. If you can't find anything from Wednesday onwards, you will have to start back earlier than that. I also want the CCTV checked in all the bars, restaurants and shops. We really need to know the last movements of this couple and who, if anyone, they have met up with. As this is proving a difficult case, the Sussex police have said that they would like to do a public appeal on television and are preparing to ask the son. He is only nineteen but he is a sensible lad and I think he will be able to deal with a television appearance. We will combine it with a female officer dressed in something stylish and red walking down the street past The Old Smithy. Because the jacket is quite unusual, it may jog someone's memory. We don't know when they went missing or where they went missing from. Finally, the Tamworth's computer,' he drew a breath and paused, 'the Sussex team have interrogated it extensively and it seems that' he paused again, 'the Tamworth's had another side to them. Yes, they were a doting couple with two lovely, well-adjusted teenagers but it appears from the websites that they visited that they were swingers.'

He paused again and the team who were beginning to tire with the length of Freeman's summary, suddenly took notice and sat up, 'Yes, swingers. Perhaps that is our link and clue here. The team are still working on the computer and are looking for some kind of current link to someone out there. Sheila, I would like you to do our street reconstruction. Please dress in something red and appropriate and we will do this after the six o'clock news this evening, in an attempt to jog someone's memory. How is it going with the hospital checks?' Freeman turned to the relevant officers who had been visiting the hospitals.

'Nothing at all, boss, and we have also checked with traffic and they have no records of any incident involving a blue Auris with that registration number.'

There was a look of dismay around the room, as the team realised that there were no fresh leads today. They would have to hope that something would come from the public television appeal and the reconstruction at The Old Smithy, this evening. A blue Auris could not be found but a similar car, in blue was collected from a colleague and Sheila was sent home to prepare herself to look as much like Mrs Tamworth as possible.

Mike and Patrick set off in order to conduct their door to door enquiries along Bury Street. 'We will have to find something out today, somebody must have seen or heard something!' Mike said as they climbed into their unmarked car and set off for Liskeard.

When they arrived, they drove straight to The Bay Tree Hotel where the Bartholomews had spent the night and told them that they could return to The Old Smithy.

'Not a bad hotel, I suppose, but I'm pleased we can go back. It'll be a bit strange after seeing those forensic people there,' Rita was heard to say to her husband as they climbed into the back of the car.

'You may see a public appeal on the six o'clock news this evening, in relation to this incident which involves a missing couple. We will be conducting a reconstruction in the street immediately after with a police officer dressed to look like one of the couple.' Patrick said to them, as they drove the short distance back to the cottage.

DCI Freeman and DC Soloman had delegated the jobs to their team. Photographs of the Tamworths had been given out to the team members.

'If we don't get a lead soon,' Freeman started, 'we may have to produce posters of the Tamworths, so our job today,' he said continuing on to Soloman, 'is to prepare for this evening and then take phone calls afterwards from the general public. Draw up a rota for the team this evening, so we are covered through the night. Make sure you put yourself on the first section so that you can be gone by nine o'clock. I'll start at five am so that I can collate all the information into a briefing for tomorrow's meeting, first thing at eight am.'

Soloman did as he was asked and then telephoned Richard with the news that he would not be back until after nine o'clock. He could meet up for a snack between four and five. He would look forward to leaving the headquarters for a break. The police building was new and despite air conditioning it always seemed to be stuffy.

The preparations continued and Sheila rang in to say that she had been to the hairdressers and had gone to the trouble and expense of having a similar haircut as Bridget Tamworth, complete with pink streaks. She had searched through her wardrobe and found a low cut red silk blouse and a red jacket. It was the best that she could do. She understood her brief and was ready to be collected in the blue car.

On the local news at six o'clock, there was an extensive report which lasted for almost fifteen minutes. Later, the main news ran a similar report. Both showed the seriousness with which the police were taking the situation. A telephone number was displayed continuously throughout. Simon Tamworth made a genuine plea for the public's help in locating their parents. His sister Vanessa sat beside him but understandably did not say anything. It was a most heartfelt request and the production team were very pleased with his efforts.

At seven o'clock a blue Ford Focus drove very slowly into Bury Street. It drove the full length whereupon it stopped and Sheila got out. With her new hairstyle and sporting a short skirt, red blouse and jacket and strappy sandals with four inch heels, she created quite a stir in the street. Despite these being her own clothes, she had advised her colleagues that she wouldn't normally wear them together in this combination. She teetered along the street aware that others were looking at her. Her brief was to do an about-turn at the end of the road and repeat the process. She was to go into any shops that were open and browse. The shop owners and staff had been advised about what was happening and who she was.

In the small convenience store, there was an altercation between a woman and Sheila by the small chest freezer containing bags of frozen peas. The woman, who was a local, had seen the news and popped out for some frozen vegetables to add to her husband's dinner. She had become slightly confused as she thought that

Sheila was the real missing woman. She had rushed to the counter and demanded that the doors be locked and that the police be called. The manager and Sheila pacified her eventually and took her into the storeroom where Sheila produced her warrant card. Even after this, she still left the shop muttering that she had seen the 'real' missing woman.

Sheila managed to return to the blue car without any further altercations and she and the driver returned to the police headquarters. It was decided that she would repeat the reconstruction tomorrow morning at eleven o'clock and then again at three in the afternoon.

Half an hour later, the special phone lines started ringing. Soloman monitored the calls with Mike. There were a few supposed sightings but certainly nothing concrete. One of the shop workers had remembered a woman fitting the description coming in and buying bread, milk and a newspaper. She hadn't been wearing the now infamous red jacket, not at nine am. Dates, times and places were all recorded but sadly nothing new was gleaned. Soloman read the notes that were being made and realised that the phone calls merely proved that the Tamworths had been in the area, staying at The Old Smithy, at the time they were booked in for.

Back in Chichester, Simon and Vanessa desperately waited for news of their parents. Vanessa was very distressed and sat rocking on the sofa. The police liaison officer became more concerned and made a note of her mood. Sharon and her mother were still giving her a lift to school but as the days passed, her teachers began to notice that she became more withdrawn and distant. She had a glazed look in her eye and although there was a smile eventually, she didn't seem to be in the present. It was as if she was far away, somewhere else. She did speak to Simon but only about day-to-day issues. The fears and worries that she had, she kept to herself.

Simon continued to go into work. He told himself that he needed to keep up a routine. Both his boss, David and the motherly, Karen, noticed that he was withdrawing and was not his usual cheerful self. They were not surprised.

Ore Soloman eventually arrived home a little later than expected. The phone lines hadn't been busy but it had been a long day and he was grateful for the short distance home. As he went through the door, he was greeted by more homely cooking smells and a cheery voice saying, 'dinner in ten minutes, so you had better get that cute little arse into the shower,' and then a little softer, 'lovely to see you home O, you've earned this,' handing him a large gin and tonic.

Ore headed towards the bathroom and realised that despite it having been a difficult day and tiring mentally and physically, he felt contented and peaceful. His arrival home had never been as lovely and comforting as it was with Richard being there with a meal on the table and a gin and tonic thrust into his hand as he came through the door.

Better hold onto this one he thought. It's good to know a hotelier.

Despite the difficult case, in which there didn't seem to be any headway, he felt at ease and relaxed. He would be able to switch off from the events of the day and concentrate on another lovely evening with Richard.

There was a stillness in the air. The previously chattering birds were silenced and the atmosphere became stuffy. The evening turned into night. The temperatures remained warm and the wine flowed.

Chapter 12

Richard and Ore lay in bed talking. It was far too hot for sleeping. They lay there under the large roof window which portrayed the black night sky.

'Do you think it might rain?' Ore said, wishing it was a bit cooler.

'It might,' came a sleepy reply.

'I'm going to open the window. I must get some sleep. I have another busy day again tomorrow.'

Ore climbed out of bed and walked over to the window that overlooked the fields at the back. Nothing moved outside and he could just make out the cows which were all lying down. All was quiet and peaceful. It was as if the world was waiting for something to happen. Eventually sleep came to them both.

Two hours later, they were both woken by an enormous clap of thunder. A minute after that there was a catastrophic flash of lightning. It broke the night sky in two and the flash plunged sharply downwards into the field behind. Then another clap of thunder but this time it was further away.

'Just what I need,' Ore said now wide awake.

Then the rain commenced. It poured down in such great quantities that the gutters immediately filled and the water cascaded over the edges.   Then another flash of lightning and ten seconds later another clap of thunder. They had slept through the first enormous flash but Richard was also now wide awake. He climbed out of bed and peered through the window. It was hard to see as the glass was covered in continuous rivulets of water.

'I love a good storm.'

'I'm not so keen, I'm going to make tea,' Ore said.

The storm raged on and the rain kept falling with such force and magnitude that the car park began to fill with water. Three car alarms had started with horns blaring and accompanied by orange flashing indicators. Ore, with his police head on, began to think of the ensuing traffic problems that all the extra water on the roads would create.

It was now four thirty and very soon it would begin to get light. The air felt a little less stuffy. The storm had left behind a better atmosphere and it was now cooler.
Having drunk the tea and tried to read his book, Ore had gone back to bed. The excitement of the storm was over and within ten minutes they were both fast asleep. The rain however kept falling.

Despite the fact that there had been no rain for a whole month, the water did not dissipate and large puddles formed in the car park below Ore's flat. It also flowed in great torrents down the streets and lanes, across the fields and down off the moors. The blocked drains and hardened earth had seen to that. Debris and dirt created mayhem and problems for many as day broke.

There had been a weather warning but the recent good weather had lulled everyone into a false sense of security. No one had really believed it or taken it seriously.

The next morning, despite the noise of the storm Ore awoke feeling inwardly calm.

He showered, eat his breakfast and saying goodbye to Richard, who still lay in bed, he made his way to work.

Chapter 13

DCI Freeman had not slept well again. Not only was he concerned about his dear wife and the imminent birth of their second child but he also had this case to solve. It was reluctant to reveal any clues and his weekly review on progress with his boss, Superintendent Louise Marshall, was looming on the Monday.

The violent storm the night before had kept the Freeman household awake and his young daughter had needed much comforting. At the first clap of thunder, she had screamed. Despite the drawn curtains in her bedroom, the pretty pink walls had been lit up with frightening brightness and clarity. At every clap of thunder and lightning strike, she screamed in terror and Gavin had spent several hours sitting with her. She had insisted on her favourite story being read, over and over, after the storm had abated for a complete hour. Finally, as dawn broke she slept.

There had been no point in Gavin going back to his own bed, as he had promised to go into work for five o'clock, to collate information gleaned from the phone calls.

He telephoned his wife in hospital to see how her night had been. She had lain in bed with a cooling flannel over her forehead, such was the heat of the night. She had not slept at all and was now tired, hot, frustrated and in quite considerable discomfort. She begged Gavin to come and sit with her but he told her that as much as he wanted to, he really had to concentrate on this case. 'What on earth can be more important?' she had screamed at him. He promised to leave whatever he was doing as soon as their baby was on the way, but in the meantime, she would have to make do with his mother for support.

Sadly, as a result of the police reconstruction and television news appeal, there had been no new information and the phone calls had only confirmed what they already knew about the Tamworths.

The team in Chichester, who were analysing their computer, were still trying to find a possible link between their disappearance and their links to swinger websites. Nothing was forthcoming.

DCI Freeman gathered the team together and started his summary as a reminder to all. Today the team were going to follow up and check the house to house results and anything further that came from any phone calls. Sheila was ready to proceed with her reconstruction walk again at eleven o'clock that morning and again at three o'clock in a vain effort to retrieve something valuable from someone's memory.

In the next room, Jessica Bellingham was taking calls from persons ringing about either the reconstruction or the television appeal. At nine o'clock, she answered a call and a female voice with a strong Cornish accent spoke, 'I've just come in from my walk. I always do it at this time with Charlie, he's my cockapoo. Anyhow, we were walking along the coast path, as we always do, when I look over the cliff edge and see something bright red on the beach below. It's only a little cove with rocks and you can't get to it from the top, so I was wondering if it was that red jacket that was mentioned on the television.

'Thank you for ringing in with this information. Let's start with your name and address and then perhaps you can explain where it was that you took Charlie for his walk this morning.'

'Pet Tarn,' came the reply, 'that's short for Petula but everyone calls me Pet. I live in Tintagel and we walk past the castle towards Trebarwith Strand on the coast path. It was one of those coves just past the church.'

Pet gave her address and Jessica finalised the call, 'we will be in touch and send someone around to see you today. Stay at home please, until we have visited you.'

As soon as she had finished the call, Jessica took this new and potentially vital piece of information into the meeting and handed the notes to Freeman.

Immediately the meeting finished, DCI Freeman called the Coastguard Search and Rescue. Jessica was to call the ambulance service and the RNLI.

'We have to hope Pet Tarn has seen something of relevance,' Soloman said as they ran down the stairs to Freeman's car, ten minutes later.

The ambulance service was to meet them by the church, once the exact spot had been ascertained and the lifeboat was dispatched from Port Isaac. It was to wait under the cliffs near the church for further instructions.

DCI Freeman and DC Soloman's journey was slow due to the torrential amount of rain that had fallen. Cars had been abandoned and the traffic division was busy dealing with several serious accidents. On two occasions they were re-routed due to fallen branches and flooded roads.

Eventually, an hour later and with the temperature rising, they stood knocking on Pet Tarn's front door. They persuaded her to accompany them, to show them which little cove she had seen the red object. The heat and dampness were making the day uncomfortable. Freeman's shirt was sticking to his back and this together with his lack of sleep began to make him irritable.

Pet had always had a dog and had trained them all to obey her commands. They respected this and as a result were well-behaved. Charlie was no exception and loved the company that these two men provided. Soloman was slightly wary of him at first but having sat in the back of the car with him, whilst Pet in the front had directed Freeman, he had decided that Charlie was harmless. Charlie had even nuzzled up to Soloman on the back seat and decided that he was a new friend.

We can't go any further than this,' Pet exclaimed. 'It is too uneven. We will have to walk from here.'

Freeman parked the car and they all set off along the coast path. The sun shone down from a brilliant blue sky creating a glittering effect on the calm sea. It was turning into a beautiful day and they were grateful for the cooling sea breeze.

Overnight the once dry and firm coast path, had turned into a mud bath and Freeman, Soloman, Pet and Charlie slipped and slid along the track.

The ambulance was already parked by the church and as they walked along Pet Tarn began to look anxious and nervous. She wasn't used to such responsibility and whilst the phone call had been relatively easy, it was now much harder being in the company of important policemen. Could she remember exactly which cove it was? Charlie trudged willingly along at their sides, grateful for his extra walk.

'It's this one,' Pet exclaimed with complete certainty, holding just a bit too firmly onto DCI Freeman's hand, as she peered over the edge. They all looked and far below   there was definitely something red but it was hard to see exactly what it was.

Freeman and Soloman both looked through binoculars. Charlie had been ordered to lie quietly on the grass on the land side of the path.

'It's definitely worth a closer look,' Freeman exclaimed at last and promptly called the RNLI, to despatch themselves from their position to the cove and investigate further.

Twenty minutes later the orange boat came into view but because of the rocks, it could not dock or send in the smaller on-board craft. It therefore reluctantly turned around and returned to Port Isaac.

'Call the helicopter!' he barked at Soloman. 'I want them to winch a man down to those rocks and take a proper look.'

Soloman did as he was asked.

'And whilst we are waiting,' Freeman continued hurriedly, 'ring the station and find out how Sheila got on with her reconstruction.'

Freeman turned to Pet, 'thanks for all your help and for coming with us. We will take it from here. There's no need for you to stay. Do you need a lift back?'

Freeman was keen to dispatch Pet Tarn back to her bungalow, just in case there was a broken body on the rocks below. If there was, they would have to investigate how it had arrived there, and whether it was relevant to their missing persons.

Pet looked aggrieved at the suggestion that she should now leave, just when things were becoming more interesting. First the rescue boat and now the helicopter and it wasn't even lunch time yet.

'Can't I stay? There must be something I can do to help.'

'It's kind of you to offer but I really need this area cleared and all those surplus to requirements to leave the vicinity.'

He gestured to Pet that she really did need to be on her way.

67

'Come on Charlie, we can see when we are not needed.'

Charlie obediently got up and together the pair set off up the path retracing their earlier steps.

'I need another team here,' Soloman heard Freeman say, as he spoke to the Bodmin headquarters. We may be onto something and I need this area cordoned off and the coast path rerouted around what might be a crime scene.

'How did Sheila get on?' Freeman said turning to Soloman, who was now pacing up and down a short section of the immediate coast path.

'Much the same as yesterday, boss. She did it this time without interruption and all went according to plan. She's back at the station now, helping to monitor any calls.'

Freeman appeared disinterested, as there was nothing more positive to add. But just then, the sound of whirring rotor blades made them look up and out to sea. Gradually the red and white coastguard helicopter became larger until it hovered over the edge of the cliff, near to where they were standing. The increased air flow made them all sit down and it provided extra relief from the now burning midday sun.

Immediately a crew member was winched to the rocks below and Freeman and Soloman waited with bated breath. But the rocks below were not a stable place to land. The very high tides, from the storm the night before, had washed up all manner of debris. There was a huge quantity of seaweed making the rocks a slippery nightmare. It was everywhere and there were also plastic bottles, pieces of wood and polystyrene which had all been thrown up on the upper part of this little cove. It really was no more than a small inlet.

At first the red item was not immediately apparent at ground level. But with the help of a number of gesticulations from Freeman and

Soloman from above, who were leaning precariously over the edge, the red item of interest was found. The man at the bottom of the rope was winched over and bent down to examine it further. Freeman and Soloman saw him pick it up and put it down. The winched man looked up and gave a thumbs down sign. Picking up the red item, he gave the appropriate signal to be lifted backup and soon he was standing on the cliff edge with Soloman and Freeman, holding a red sheet of plastic and some rope that had been wrapped around it.

Freeman's face was a picture of disappointment.

'Not of any interest to us.' Soloman confirmed the situation.

At that moment, two police constables arrived having walked from the church. They both looked hot and tired.

'Where shall we cordon off this area from and to?' the first one said.

'False alarm,' Soloman replied, 'no crime scene here after all.'

'Make yourself useful,' Freeman said, 'put this in the nearest bin. It's no use to us.'

He handed the plastic sheet and rope to the police constables and within five minutes, the helicopter had left the scene and the police presence had returned back along the   path.

The coast path walkers, who had been held up at the stiles at either end of this section above the cove, were now free to resume walking. There had been much surmising as to what had been going on. 'A possible incident,' was all that they had been told.

'Can't always expect every lead to take us forward,' Soloman calmly said, trying to dissipate Freeman's obvious anxiety. The build-up of his lack of sleep and the heat were not helping his mood.

'You realise,' Freeman said to Soloman, changing the subject completely, 'that I may have to go off at any minute if the baby arrives, so from now on, we take both cars.'

The journey back to Bodmin was carried out in silence. Both were thinking about the day's activities and what should happen next.

Chapter 14

When Ore arrived home later that evening, he found that Richard had organised to have pizza delivered. He appreciated how well he was being looked after. He was hoping upon hope, that this crazy lack of a work pattern would not put Richard off. Please, please let this work, he thought to himself.

'What's up O? You look deep in thought.' Richard had already shortened Ore's name to 'O' as a term of endearment.

'I'm just loving you being here,' he began 'but I'm so aware that I'm not really being fair to you, with my unexpected workload at the moment. I really like you, really do.' He looked sad, as if he wanted to say more.

'Work sometimes but not always has to come first. I know that from bitter experience. I am growing very fond of you too and I'm prepared to give this a go to make it work, so stop worrying and looking so sad. There's a good film on in a minute and I wanted to talk with you about that art gallery in Looe. I went there today, some good stuff. I'd really like your opinion on one piece I particularly like. If you approve, I will buy it and then you can enjoy it every time you come to Clifton.'

'When I get a chance, I'd love to come and look.'

Ore managed a faint smile in recognition of Richard's kind and enthusiastic words and then just as he was beginning to feel a little more encouraged, his phone rang. As he picked it up, his heart sank. It was Freeman calling. What does he want now? He thought.

'I'm at the hospital, Becky is in labour. I don't know how long before little one will arrive; I'll keep you posted. Can you deputise for me at tomorrow's meeting?'

'Yes boss,' Ore said it without thinking but he knew that he would cope somehow and it would be an excellent time to prove himself.

'I had better go, the nurse has just arrived again.'

He hung up abruptly.

'What's up?' Richard could see the worried look on Ore's face.

'Work, and Becky has gone into labour, so Freeman has put me in charge and I'm taking the daily team meeting tomorrow. I may have to lead the main weekly meeting with the superintendent on Monday.

'It's all good experience for you O, the boss will see just how competent and confident you are.'

'Better go in early, again,' Ore replied, stressing the word 'again'. 'Which means I had better get some shut eye, a hug would be nice though.'

It was an uneventful night. No electric storms or flash flooding meant that Richard and Ore and the population of Cornwall had a peaceful sleep.

Meanwhile in Chichester, Simon and Vanessa were experiencing yet another restless night. Simon was trying to hold it all together but increasingly his thoughts were turning from 'where are they?' to 'what has happened?'

Vanessa was her usual quiet self but Simon knew that holding it all in was not a good idea. We'd better have a chat over the weekend, Simon thought. Perhaps I'll take Karen up on her offer and invite her round.

He arranged this with her on the following morning, for Sunday, when he knew that he wasn't working and Vanessa would be at home.

Chapter 15

The next morning dawned sunny and bright and although it looked like it might be another warm day, there was a freshness in the air. When Soloman left his flat at seven thirty, he noticed how the previously dry and dusty grass had begun to look greener after the torrents of rain from two nights before. It was a comfortable walk into work and he remembered that today he would definitely be using his car, which was parked at the station.

There had been no further communication from Freeman regarding the birth of his baby. They all knew that he was at his wife's hospital bedside.

He made his way to his desk and dialled the number for DCI Willoughby at West Sussex police.

'We need to speak with Simon and Vanessa,' he said desperately, 'despite all our efforts and many hours having been given to this case by a large team, we are not making any break throughs. This happens every time we think we are achieving something. We've done news items, appeals, street reconstructions and dedicated phone lines but still nothing is coming to light.'

Soloman laid their efforts on thickly. He did not want West Sussex division believing that Devon and Cornwall couldn't handle the case. He also did not want to let Freeman or the rest of the team down. This was all good experience for him and he was grateful for the challenges.

DCI Willoughby was very helpful and supportive that morning.

'That's no problem, I'll phone them myself, straightaway. I was going to call you after the weekend to see how it was going. I'm sorry that the whereabouts of the Tamworths is still a mystery. I'll be in touch when I have arranged the telephone interview.'

Having hung up, Willoughby dialled the number for the leisure centre, hoping that Simon was on duty and having been called to the phone, Simon agreed to speak to Soloman straight away. His pool duties were light that afternoon and he was pleased that at last someone from the Devon and Cornwall Police wanted to update him. It had been four days since his original call.

Within ten minutes Simon was again being tannoyed to come to the front reception.

'Good afternoon, I am DC Soloman and you are Simon Tamworth?'

'Yes, that's me, Simon replied. 'Have you found them?'

'I'm afraid we haven't and that's the real reason for the call, to see if there is anything else that you can tell us, the slightest thing. At the moment, despite all our efforts and I can assure you that every priority has been made to try and ascertain the whereabouts of your parents, we are coming up against a brick wall each time we think we might be onto something.'

'Vanessa and I have been thinking all week,' Simon replied. There was a note of disappointment in his voice. 'My mother in some respects was a bit old fashioned in that for many years she kept a diary. I have had a look through them, I shouldn't have I suppose. All I can find is.'…… There was a long hesitation.

'Go on Simon,' Soloman said breaking the silence, 'whatever it is, I will have heard or seen it before.'

'Well the thing is, these diaries are at least ten years old, and there are no current ones. They use the computer now but there are references at weekends to meeting people, people I have no recollection of but there are no names, just initials and a town. Most of the towns or villages are within a thirty mile radius of here. It doesn't make any sense to either of us at all. We didn't know anything about any of this then. We were too young and at weekends, when these meetups took place, we were always at my aunt's.'

'That seems to tie up with a theory that we are working on at the moment but is there anything else? Did anyone come to the house that you didn't know or who seemed out of place, to your family circle?'

'No, I don't remember anything. As I said we were taken to our aunt's some weekends and then as we grew older, we were allowed to stay at home by ourselves.'

'Were you ever given an explanation for being taken to your aunt's? How often did it occur?'

'About once a month and no, we were just told aunty enjoyed seeing us as she had no children of her own.'

'And latterly, when you were at home at weekends, did you not think that rather odd?'

'We were just used to spending one weekend a month without our parents, though thinking about it now and having spoken to other people, we both realise that it is not the norm. Do you know what is going on?'

'I can't say at present, the relevant departments are working very hard and hopefully we will have some more leads soon that we can follow up. I will come back to you directly, when we find anything out, please be assured of that.'

Simon and DC Soloman said their goodbyes and the call was ended.

Not much new gleaned from that call, Soloman thought and he was just updating the case notes, when George and Hilary veered around the partition of his desk and without stopping said, 'Freeman's baby has been born. It's a little boy, just about two hours ago, and all is well with Becky.'

Soloman saw the cans of lager in their hands. He hadn't seen this pair on his team acting like this before.

'We are celebrating then.'

'Of course,' came back an exuberant reply.

Soloman finished what he was doing and then joined the others, where he too was handed a can.

'Bit early isn't it?' he found himself saying and then realised he had well and truly slipped into Freeman's role.

'It is Saturday and there isn't much going on,' came back the reply from Hilary.

'I've just been speaking to an exhausted nineteen year old who is worried sick about his parents and you stand there and tell me that there isn't much going on.'

Soloman quite surprised himself. If Freeman had been there, he would have been joining in without any encouragement. But Freeman was not there and he was taking charge.

'Another five minutes and then we had better get back to it guys. There are all these links to possible leads that the IT department have just released. They all need checking out and possibly visiting. I want you all to work through the list, many of whom may be swingers who have met up with the Tamworths. We should sober up and spend the rest of the day doing this. How we get on will dictate whether we continue tomorrow.'

'Well, it's got to be said,' Soloman said, turning to Mike and Patrick who were both looking rather amazed at this turnaround in their team member.

'I have to justify everything on Monday, to the superintendent.'

Fifteen minutes later the mood in the office changed. Coffee had been made and the previous frivolity and high mood had disappeared. Instead of laughter and happy voices, there was now the constant sound of keyboards being operated and talking in hushed tones.

They worked soundly through the rest of the day. Calls were made and copious notes were taken. Alibis were given for the previous week and it became apparent that only two couples might have had contact with the Tamworths.

The first couple were H and D Wilkins from Portsmouth and the second, R and S Davidson from Worthing. Freeman and Soloman would have to visit both couples, investigate and determine their involvement.

There wasn't much information on the Tamworth's computer, he discovered a mobile number with "R and S, Worthing" and an email address for "H and D, Portsmouth." The team would have to search harder to find addresses.

After this he decided that there wasn't much more he could do that day. Reluctantly he felt that in Freeman's absence, he should work for a few hours the next day, to try and push ahead with these two new leads. In the meantime, he would go home, for it would be his last evening with Richard.

Ore arrived home fifteen minutes later. It was a warm Saturday evening and he was happy. He had left behind his work and with lovely thoughts of an evening with Richard, it was as if a work switch had been turned to off.

Visions of a drive to the coast and a meal or a drink at a beach bar, followed by a leisurely walk filled his mind. The smell of the sea, sand between his toes and the sound of waves were all memories from a few nights before that he wanted to experience again.

He hadn't managed to communicate with Richard all day, unlike previous days and was feeling slightly guilty. The guilt of having to work all week hadn't disappeared and he was still disappointed that he had in effect been trumped by the birth of a baby. This case had appeared just prior to the birth and the whole week had been a mess. His disappointment turned to annoyance but he quickly rationalised that if he really wanted this job, he would have to accept these situations.

He turned the key in the lock but unlike other days, when he had been greeted by a lovely smile, a big hug and shortly afterwards a large gin and tonic, his flat was empty. No sound stirred and there were no heavenly cooking aromas. All was neat and tidy. All the washing up had been done and as he looked around, he saw a note on the kitchen worktop.

As he went forward to read it, his mind was saying that it would read

I will be back at six thirty.

But it didn't. Instead it read

Truly sorry, have had to go back to work tonight. See you tomorrow x

It must have been a bit of a crisis, he thought. There was no mention of going back until Sunday evening.

He felt upset and the disappointment came back. His lovely evening had dissipated into thin air and his plans to go back into work tomorrow now conflicted directly with Richard returning. It would hardly be fair to be going out of the door just as Richard was coming back in, especially after this crisis in Bristol followed by a long drive back to Cornwall.

It had all been going so well and now it wasn't. Why was life so unfair, just when he had found the beginnings of happiness? Ore sat down and consoled himself with the thought that there was nothing more he could do but they would have a chat the next day in order to be supportive and understanding to one another.

But he could just make a quick call and this he did.

'Hi O,' he heard as Richard answered. 'I'm really sorry about this evening. I had a call at lunchtime to say that Gabriella, my deputy, had had an accident and was in hospital and couldn't run the large function that the hotel had booked in one of the suites this evening. I had to drop everything and get back here pronto, to make sure everything was in order. I'm so sorry. I'm hoping to come back tomorrow for our last day.' He paused as if waiting for confirmation that this was alright.

'These things happen I suppose. Can't say I am not disappointed. I really needed a lovely night off. I have to go in tomorrow; we have a few leads which we must follow up immediately. I can go in, in the morning or leave it to the afternoon?'

Ore's question did not get answered.

'Have to go now,' he heard Richard say. 'I will see you in the morning.

80

From the tone in Richard's voice, Ore felt relatively assured. Tomorrow will just unfold as it happens, he thought. I can't do more than that.

After beans on toast, a shower and an hour of television, Ore went to bed. Eventually he fell asleep. It was another warm night.

He was awakened at seven thirty by birdsong outside his window. He usually slept with them open and the hedges around the fields below, provided the birds with shelter. They had been awake for hours. The sun rise and dawn chorus had been and gone several hours before.

Ore looked at the empty space in his bed and realised that he missed Richard very much. How quickly he had become accustomed to him being there.

He lay there thinking about how to plan the day ahead. But he couldn't get past what time he thought Richard would arrive back. Perhaps if he got up now and went straight into work, he would be back before Richard arrived. He calculated that it would take a minimum of two hours to drive back down from Bristol. That was feasible early on a Sunday morning with less traffic and good conditions. He would have to drive at some speed though. However, he would have had a late night and might not be back until lunchtime. Ore decided to get up and go to work straight away.

He threw back the duvet and made his way to the bathroom. Having brushed his teeth and after a quick shower, he went into the kitchen and put the kettle on. Reaching for the cafetiere, he heard the sound of a key in the lock and to his complete amazement and surprise, there in front of him as the door opened was Richard.

After a long hug, Richard explained that he had had a few hours of sleep and then decided that he would drive down early to make the most of the day. Despite his travels, and running a function, he still managed to look fabulous. Chino shorts and a smart white T shirt adorned his brown body.

They stood there smiling at one another.

'I can't believe it. You're here. I'm so pleased.' It was all that Ore could say.

'Ah, I've got something for you, just to make up for last night and not being here. I've left it outside the door.'

He reappeared through the door, a second later with a huge floral arrangement.

'Just for you,' he said, handing it over.

Ore was speechless. No one had ever bought him flowers before. In fact, he hadn't ever considered receiving flowers as a gift. But then as he took them and saw the care and attention that someone had obviously taken in their presentation, when he took a breath of the scent and marvelled at the colours, he was truly grateful.

'Thank you,' was all he was able to muster, 'but how did you manage to get hold of these? It's a Sunday morning.'

'When you are in the hotel business, one quickly learns that one has to be able to attempt to put things right at a moment's notice. It is not what one knows, but who. I'm lucky to know a very obliging florist,' he laughed.

'They are beautiful. I was just making some coffee. Do you want some?'

'Certainly do, I'll just have a quick shower if I may?'

'No problem.'

Fifteen minutes later Richard emerged from the bathroom and entered the kitchen.

'Are you hungry, want some breakfast?'

Richard came up behind Ore and put his arms around his waist. Peering over his shoulder, he said:

'Well just look at that, you do the same as me.'

'What, you mean lining the pan with foil, before grilling bacon?'

'Yes, precisely, my mum instilled it in me from a very young age. Heaven forbid if it wasn't adhered to.'

'That's a bit spooky. My mum is just the same. Ever since I was old enough to remember, she did it and it had to be done a certain way, folding in the corners, so that there was no way anything could escape.'

Ore turned to face Richard and they burst out laughing. Better keep up with what our mums have instilled,' Richard said most emphatically.

Bacon sandwiches and coffee were served. They sat and discussed their jobs and the need to be versatile, no matter how hard or inconvenient.

An hour later, after they had solemnly agreed that work would have to come first, at this stage, they also agreed that when they had time off, they would go away, perhaps on a city break in Europe, so that they would get a proper rest.

'Better get off to work then,' Ore finally said. 'I'll only be a few hours.'

Fifteen minutes later, having walked to the Police headquarters, Soloman was standing by his desk. Although a Sunday, Mike and Patrick were there.

'Any news from Hampshire or West Sussex?' Soloman asked.

83

'Nothing as yet boss. It was only yesterday that we came across these two couples.'

'I have a meeting with the Superintendent in the morning. I need to be able to tell her that we have made substantial progress, especially as Freeman is away. Get onto them again and make sure that they understand the need for a thorough internet search of all the relevant websites and swingers clubs. I've had a brief look and there are quite a few locally and even more in London. Start with the local ones before you move onto London. They should check all their records for anyone with these initials. If we can at least find these people, then we can get them checked out and I will have something positive for the Superintendent. There is nothing to stop us checking also, so please divide up the work and start searching yourselves.'

Soloman was feeling the weight of the case on his shoulders. Turning to his desk, he attempted to concentrate on his own work. He set about collecting everything that he and the team had done since the case had begun. There had been the opening case file with all the information from DCI Willoughby and DC Oliver-Jones. There had been the reconstruction walks, the television appeal by Simon and Vanessa, the door to door inquiries and Pet Tarn believing that she had seen something red and relevant. There had been the discovery of the holiday cottage that had been used by the missing guests and the ensuing search of the property. Now there would soon be investigations into various clubs.

He knew how important it was not to let down any member of the team. He was enjoying this new responsibility but not in a better than you manner. It was more that he was finding that he was perfectly capable of taking on the challenges and sometimes complex thought processes. He mustn't let Freeman or the Superintendent down either. He was also hoping that Freeman would not be back too soon.

The birth of Freeman's son had passed without incident. Mother and baby were doing well and would be going home that same day. At the start of this case, with the pending birth imminent, Freeman had drawn Soloman to one side and promised that if the birth had gone well, then he would delay his paternity leave until later. His mother could look after his wife and daughter. He was therefore due back tomorrow, Monday, and could be brought back up to speed with the case.

He was nearly finished, when Mike appeared at the side of his desk.

'We might have something definite here, just discovered a couple with the same initials, R and S, who belong to a club in Brighton.'

'Excellent news,' Soloman exclaimed, 'I'll go tomorrow with Freeman after the meeting first thing. Get the club address for us and arrange a Travel Lodge for the night. Hopefully you will have the same success with the couple from Portsmouth.'

Soloman gave Mike a look which implied that he expected results with the second couple imminently but he managed to say it with a note of kindness in his voice.

'We will have to start calling you Freeman Two,' Mike said with a big smile.

Both knew and understood the joke. Freeman was good at keeping the impetus up with his team.

Soloman finished his preparations and told the team that he would be leaving shortly. He would continue early the next day.

Chapter 16

It was mid-afternoon when Ore Soloman emerged from the Police Headquarters. The sun shone and there was a calmness in the air. It was a beautiful time of day. Even the traffic was hushed and everywhere there was the smell of food cooking on barbeques. The inhabitants of Cornwall and the visiting holiday-makers had been lulled by the beauty and tranquillity of the day. Those that had travelled to join other family members across the county had long since arrived at their destinations. The shops in the towns and villages were beginning to close up and families and friends were enjoying themselves and relaxing.

The beaches, however, were busy and the seaside cafes thronged with thirsty tea drinkers and families wanting a cream tea. The bars were also busy with beer and wine drinkers, especially those on the coast.

Ore hurried along the deserted pavement and up the road to his flat. He was pleased to see Richard's car parked in the visitor's bay. Hopefully they would be able to go out immediately and enjoy this lovely afternoon. Richard was sitting on the balcony enjoying the sunshine and the view across the fields.

'I have a picnic all packed and ready to go,' he said getting to his feet from the sun lounger. 'It's a fantastic spot this, not overlooked at all and it seems to get the sun most of the day. It's very peaceful and with an interesting view.'

'Yes, that's partly why I moved here,' Ore replied, 'I'll just change and then we can go. Looe or somewhere else, where do you fancy?'

'Oh definitely the seaside, Looe will be fine.'

The rest of the afternoon followed in a kind of dreamy summery haze, as if they were in the middle of a water colour painting, where the artist had been very generous with the water and all the colours seemed to have run together.

The traffic was light and they soon found a parking place. Someone else had just been leaving.

'Shame for them, lovely for us.' Ore remarked.

They walked to the end of the beach and found a quiet spot behind a large rock save only for the seagulls whose cries and screeching never ceased. The sound from the waves was, however, calming and restful. The tide was out and the golden sand was dry.

After they had eaten their picnic and drunk the wine, they settled down for a few hours of sunbathing.

'Have to make the most of this lovely weather. You never know when it might end.' Ore said, resting his foot on Richard's ankle.

But all good things come to an end and very reluctantly they packed up a short while later. They talked about the last time they had been there and how they had enjoyed walking on the beach and looking in the art gallery window.

'We'll have a look in there on another day,' Richard said reading Ore's mind.

The beach was beginning to empty now and the bars were becoming more crowded.

'You have to leave lovely things and places, in order to be able to visit and experience again. Such is life, I am afraid,' Richard knowingly said. 'I had an aunt who used to say that to me.'

As they neared Bodmin and the flat, a feeling of despondency descended on the pair. Soon they would have to part, temporarily and resume their work lives.

After a long embrace and a kiss goodbye, Richard drove off and Ore looked around his flat. He looked at the beautiful flowers that Richard had brought that morning.

He packed a small overnight bag ready for his intended overnight stay in Brighton the following evening and having received a message from Richard to say that he was safely home, he retired to bed and fell asleep almost immediately. Tomorrow was another day.

Chapter 17

Even though he had fallen asleep straight away, Ore Soloman did not sleep well. It was warm and humid and the air was close despite the window being open. He awoke several times in the night. Try as he might and turning over many times, he only managed to doze. His thoughts alternated between Richard and his meeting the following morning with his Superintendent. His tiredness created a mixed jumble of thoughts as is sometimes the case in life, when something new, important and exciting occurs, as in this instance with Richard. He tried to concentrate on lovely thoughts of him in order to fall asleep.

At four am he got up and wandered out onto the balcony with a glass of water. Richard had been correct. The balcony was not overlooked at all. He sat down on one of the loungers and placed his head on the back rest. His mind kept returning to thoughts of the following day. Would their trip to Brighton lead them to a successful outcome? Despite the warmth a cooling breeze had arrived and after twenty minutes he made his way back through the balcony door to his bedroom where he finally fell asleep.

His alarm woke him rudely at seven o'clock and he dutifully and robotically threw back the duvet and headed for the shower. He felt exhausted and the streaming lukewarm water did little to wake him up. He hardly noticed the stunning floral arrangement that seemed to take up most of one of his living room surfaces.

After his muesli and coffee, he set off down the road towards the Police Headquarters. The sun shone again and the birds sang. A few seagulls squawked overhead. The journey took just five minutes in the car. With his tiredness that morning he was grateful that he did not have to walk.

He was hoping that Freeman would be in early so that he could catch up with him before the meeting but his plans did not materialise as he wanted.

He met Superintendent Louise Marshall on the stairs.

'I've come in early too. Glad to see you. I'd like to have our usual weekly meeting now and then you can update the team afterwards. Can you come to my office now?'

DC Soloman knew that he would have to say yes, even though his intention had been to check if there had been any progress during the night. Having found there to be no further developments, he made his way to the Superintendent's office.

Louise Marshall was not impressed.

'How can an adult couple go missing? You tell me that there is no sign of their car and now over a week has gone by, since they left their holiday cottage. We cannot forget that this is one of the most closely watched countries in the world. The press are already having a field day and if we don't find something soon, the tourist board will have something to say. Has nothing come of Sheila's reconstruction walks? Somebody, somewhere must know something, or is hiding someone.' She carried on a little more gently, as she realised that perhaps she was being unfair on DC Soloman. 'I can see that you and the team have worked very hard but I'm afraid it's just not enough. We must get some photographic posters of the Tamworths put up everywhere. Tell Simon and Vanessa we have to do this and then get the team to implement it. I want them along both coast paths, north and south, in shops, public buildings, pubs and restaurants, anywhere that we can get access. Someone, somewhere, knows something! That's it for now. Tell the team that whilst I appreciate all their efforts, more needs to be done.'

DC Soloman left the Superintendent's office feeling slightly jaded, as she did have a point.

Chapter 18

Soloman gathered together the team and imparted the superintendents views on how the case was proceeding. Long faces and mumbles around the room followed. He finished the meeting fifteen minutes later, having organised them to create the posters of the Tamworths. Sheila was to check again with the traffic division for any accidents involving a blue Auris and also the hospitals, to check if the Tamworths had subsequently been admitted. The CCTV in the bars, restaurants and shops were to be checked again.

At that moment a breathless Jessica came hurrying towards him down the corridor.

'I am glad that I have found you, I have just taken a call from a Howard Lewis. He is on holiday with his wife and two children and has seen the item on the news. He remembers seeing a red item in the woods near here, when they were having a picnic.'

She handed him a printed sheet with all the details of the phone call.

'Thanks, I'll deal with it,' he replied taking it from her and walking to his desk.

There was no sign of Freeman. He must be needed at home, he thought. I hope there hasn't been some sort of crisis.

He told his team about this latest development. Brighton would have to wait. He would prioritise this lead. It was good to leave the building and have a trip into the countryside after his disturbed night. He was pleased to be going out on his own as it would give him a chance to clear his head and take on board his earlier meeting with the superintendent.

The sun continued to beat down; it was going to be another hot day. The woods were only a short distance away so he wouldn't be delayed for very long.

He turned his car off the main road, into a country lane, grateful for the relative peacefulness. The road was narrow and the trees either side met overhead, providing welcome relief from the gathering heat.

He had a vague idea where he was going. It was just a short way down the road. It was good to be on his own again without Freeman. Although they got on well, they had different temperaments. Soloman was still learning how best to cope with Freeman's moods. He was very capable and had the makings of a good police officer and as such it was good for him to be working on his own initiative without his boss at his side, constantly making suggestions.

Soloman turned off the lane and onto a piece of rough ground, which locals and those in the know used for parking, before setting off on their woodland walks. There were two other vehicles and Soloman chose to park away from them on the further side. Although there were trees and bushes all around, they did not meet overhead.

He sat for a moment in the car looking at his map and the pinpoint where Mr Lewis thought he had seen the "red" item. Soloman drank from his water bottle and opened the door. He was met with a wall of midday heat. A thought crossed his mind, perhaps I could do this more comfortably and quickly if I changed into my running shorts. I will blend in better. He made a snap decision and as he changed out of his jeans, it dawned on him that this was one of the spots that Freeman had advised him about all those months ago when he first arrived. Dog walkers by day and lovers by night, had been his terminology.

Placing his phone and his warrant card into a bum bag and fastening this around his waist, he set off down the track at the back of the car parking area. Like the coast path last week, the ground underfoot was muddy and large puddles lay in every direction. A new set of deep tyre tracks, fresh this morning, were also evident and from the size and pattern of the treads, Soloman could tell that they belonged to a reasonably sized, four by four off-roading vehicle.

It was much cooler in the woods and darker too. Progress was slow as Soloman negotiated his way around the puddles and ruts. He pushed his sunglasses onto his forehead. Several times he nearly slid into a deep puddle and very quickly his trainers became caked in thick brown mud. In the distance he heard a chainsaw being operated and this broke the quietness and stillness of the woods. Just off the path, a rabbit bounded past.

He met a middle age couple with their spaniel and a polite 'good morning,' was exchanged. Up ahead and walking in the same direction was a man with a golden retriever. They reached a large clearing at the same point and the man turned ready to retrace his steps.

'Not easy going underfoot is it?' he said, looking at Soloman's footwear.

Soloman looked at his trainers. He smiled at the man. 'Yes, I wasn't expecting this mud after all the sun and recent heat.'

'I come here every morning to walk Benny and I haven't seen it this bad in ages, not since last winter. Suppose we have been spoilt with all this lovely weather. Well, better be off now, Benny will be wanting his lunch.'

With that, he set off, sliding his way back to the car park.

That accounts for the two cars, Soloman thought. He was aware that the noise from the chainsaw had died and silence resumed.

Soloman had a look around the clearing in front of him. Here and there were rustic picnic tables and benches.

What a lovely place to bring a family for a picnic, Soloman thought, understanding how Mr Lewis had brought his family here the previous Sunday.

Following the directions from Mr Lewis's phone call Soloman made his way around this idyllic spot. The grass was long and lush and the sun beamed down from directly overhead. Soloman's legs were splattered with mud by this time and he was pleased that he was wearing shorts.

Sitting down at one of the benches, he gathered his thoughts and identified his position in the clearing. From the information I have here, I should be over there, he thought, gazing over to the other side where another path entered the clearing.

Soloman set off. The trees here were less densely spaced and again they stood in lush grass. The trees were not tall, perhaps they had been planted at a later date. It was an ideal place for a more private picnic, or where lovers might meet. The sun shone down between the trees, forming pools of brightness on the grass.

It was this area that Soloman now focused on, moving methodically from one side to the other and then crossing over to the other side of the path.

He was just thinking that this would be a relaxing place to bring Richard for a picnic, when he spotted something in the far corner, before the trees became denser. Yes, his heart missed a beat, over there was something red and what looked like five to six foot long and eighteen inches in diameter. He was about twenty yards away at this stage. As he drew closer, treading very warily, he realised that whatever it was, was not as red as he first thought. Yes, it was "reddish" but not what he was expecting. It bore no resemblance to a stylish red Italian leather jacket.

He was now standing by it and realised that it was not what he was hoping for, not unless there was something inside this roll of... yes it was carpet. Gingerly he crouched down at one end and peered down the centre. It was hollow. He realised at this point that it had just been discarded probably brought here as waste but first used for a picnic. How deplorable people are, he thought, bringing their rubbish to the countryside and leaving it behind.

He checked the object in front of him, as a matter of course. Unrolling the carpet to its full extent he discovered that it was an old piece of red patterned Axminster. There was nothing inside. In one sense he was pleased, that there wasn't anything suspicious here but in another sense it meant that this possible lead had led nowhere. They were back to square one.

At least this glorious, peaceful and idyllic setting was not the scene of some horrid murder. On a personal note, Ore would still be able to come here with Richard, without any bad underlying feelings. Thoughts of a picnic with sparkling wine, lying in the sun until it went down, a warm night evolving, gazing up at the moon and stars, came to mind. His thoughts abruptly returned to his current work situation.

Then he remembered the woodmen. The operators of that chainsaw were still quiet. Soloman's naturally inquisitive mind got the better of him.

He set off in the direction that he thought that he had heard the chainsaw coming from. It soon became clear that he was on the right course. He crossed through the woods for a short distance whereupon he came across the main track, wide enough for vehicles and there in front of him were deep fresh tyre marks. He paused and heard talking and laughing.

Sounds like two voices, he thought and set off again.

Only a short distance ahead, another clearing came into view. Soloman quickened his pace back into a gentle jog.

They will have finished their break in a minute. Better get to them before they start the chainsaw again, he thought.

He reached the clearing and saw directly ahead, an old pickup truck. Small felled pines lay here and there but as Soloman took in the scene in front of him, he appreciated that there was order too. Piles of exact lengths lay neatly stacked to one side, presumably waiting for collection. As Soloman glanced around, over on the far side, sitting on a folding chair in the sunlight, he saw a naked man, talking to another man a few paces away who was shirtless and holding a beaker.

'I'm sorry to disturb your break,' Soloman began. 'I am a police officer,' he searched in his bum bag for his warrant card and held it up.

The naked man seemed completely unfazed by this intrusion into their lunch break and looked back questioningly. The other man also stopped drinking and looked over.

'Not doing anything wrong are we?' the first one said.

'No, not at all,' Soloman began. 'How you choose to spend your lunch break, here in the remoteness of these lovely woods, is no concern of mine. By the look of the colour of you, you must do this all the time. You are nearly the same colour as me.' He said this with a smile and a humorous note in his voice.

'We like to get the air to our skin,' the first man said, 'it's no fun wearing those heavy chainsaw trousers in this heat,' pointing at his clothes on a nearby log, 'been a naturist all my life and Tommy here, he's coming around to my way of thinking.'

The shirtless man nodded and smiled in agreement, but he did not speak.

'It's no bother,' Soloman said, 'I'm hardly dressed as one would expect for a policeman, but we've had a lead regarding the case of the two missing persons that you may have seen on the television, for these woods. Have you seen or heard anything suspicious that is unusual for this area? By the look of all your work you have been here for several months.' he looked around at the tidy piles of neatly sawn lengths of tree trunk.

'Yes, been here since April, been a long job, but good to have some regular long term work,' the naked man said, shifting slightly in his seat. 'But no, we ain't seen or heard anything untoward like. We knows it goes on here at night and early evening but we are gone by then. We had half term when a few families came with picnics but otherwise we just keep to ourselves and gets on with the job. The boss comes around sometimes to check on progress. He lives in the big house yonder,' he said, pointing over Soloman's head.

'I see,' Soloman said, 'keep up the good work and if you do see or hear anything that is not as it should be, please be in touch.'

Soloman handed him one of his cards and the naked man peered at it, before tucking it into the fold of his T-shirt which lay with his other clothes.

Soloman left the duo happy in their sunny work and retraced his steps down the muddy tracks to his car.

You never know how the day is going to unfold, Soloman mused to himself, especially here in Cornwall. It was a happy thought that left him smiling.

98

He put on his T-shirt, glad that he had made the choice to put his running gear in the car. He sat down and made a call back to the station, stating that the possible lead from Mr Lewis was not going to take the case forward and that there was no new evidence. Was there any news from the hospital and traffic division?

The answers were negative.

Door-to-door enquiries and CCTV checks at the bars, restaurants and shops were also drawing blanks.

He set off back to Bodmin, stopping at his flat to shower and change. He noticed the emptiness of the flat and told himself to keep busy. He briefly looked at the card that he had placed on the side table and took a moment to read the loving handwritten words inside.

I am missing you already.
Although only a short visit, I have so enjoyed your company.
Any time that we are apart is for me, too long.
I sincerely hope to see you again very soon.
My love
R x

A single tear formed in his eye. No one had ever written such lovely words to him before. He made a mental note to purchase a card and send it to Bristol, to maintain the flow. He looked at the extravagant bouquet of flowers on the side table. His only vase was just big enough.

Coming back to more immediate issues, he left his flat and made his way once again into the sunshine. He drove the short distance back to the station.

DCI Freeman had been in touch with his team informing them that his mother was unwell with a stomach upset and therefore could not be in the company of a new baby. He had been updated briefly on the case and was pleased that DC Soloman was stepping up to the mark and managing the team without him. He would be back when his mother was better.

It was decided that Mike would accompany Soloman to Brighton. If they left straight away, they would make it to the club while it was open. Soloman thought that it was strange that it was open on a Monday evening from six pm until one am.

DS Mike Jeffers and DC Ore Soloman collected their overnight bags and made their way to the canteen to collect sandwiches, crisps, drinks and chocolate bars. It was a long way to Brighton both in time and distance and as neither of them had had any lunch they decided to eat on route. They set off in Jeffers' car.

It was now mid-afternoon and both were pleased not to be travelling in the heat of the day. They decided to take the coastal route which took them through pretty villages with thatched cottages meandering their way through the Dorset countryside. It was not a route that Soloman knew but Jeffers had a sister who lived in Bournemouth. It was a journey that he undertook several times a year.

Soloman had not worked directly alongside Jeffers before. He knew him as part of the overall team and now decided to try to get to know him better. He realised that he could certainly learn from this man with his wealth of experience and knowledge.

Jeffers was more than ten years older than Soloman. He was a quiet man who diligently proceeded with the current tasks in an organised manner, taking his role very seriously. He had been in the police force since his early twenties after he had left university. After his divorce he had become something of a loner. He still lived in Bodmin in a small house on the same estate as Freeman.

'What do you make of this case?' Soloman asked after a short lull in their previous conversation.

'Not a lot happening, is there?' Jeffers replied. 'Just seem to be coming up against dead ends all the time. That can be the case with police work, having the patience to look into every lead, even the smallest detail, leaving nothing unturned. Every detail must be logged. You never know when you might need it in the future. Might be years later, or there may be a connection with something from the past, or indeed something that hasn't happened yet, in the future.'

'Not a lot of help now, is it?' Something that hasn't happened yet.' Soloman interjected.

'Well, no,' Jeffers carried on, 'but sometimes a case is temporarily put on hold when nothing comes to light and then something else, perhaps even a parking offence, triggers it all off again and the second offence helps to solve the first. I do think that at this stage we do have to be very clear that after over a week of nothing, we are looking at a serious crime here. We know that the Tamworths have not left the country, because Willoughby and Oliver-Jones collected their passports on their house visit. Not unless they have made off in a rowing boat, for a new life. I am joking of course. There is no hint or plausible reason why they should leave the country. They have a comfortable life in their new home, mortgage free, good jobs, lovely grown up children by all accounts, finances are all in order and marriage appears happy, so it's my guess that something bad has happened. I mean, when a single person goes missing, it's one thing but for two to just disappear, that's quite another. We will get to the bottom of it, trust me. We just have to keep working away.'

There was a pause, whilst Soloman digested this. It was quite a different approach to Freeman's. Jeffers seemed quietly confident that they would get to the bottom of it eventually. All in good time but that did not mean that he took his time when he was on a case, just that he was methodical. Experience had taught him that if you were diligent, the answer arrived in the end.

'I can see exactly where you are coming from,' Soloman answered eventually. 'It's just so frustrating when one keeps running down these dead ends.'

'Don't rush down that dead end so fast, that you miss the vital clue, or even a small one, on the way. You just never know how vital even the smallest detail may turn out to be and in my experience, we always get there in the end. We are so fortunate nowadays with all the technological advances and the huge leaps forward with science, that there really isn't the perfect crime anymore. Sooner or later, someone trips up and then bang, we have the lead that we have been waiting for.'

There wasn't much more that Soloman could add to this, so he just agreed and was grateful that throughout this conversation, Jeffers's driving had remained measured and well disciplined, unlike Freeman's, whom he knew would have been erratic in line with the flow of the conversation.

They are just different, Soloman thought. Both get there in the end. I will watch and learn from them both.

'This swinger idea is only a lead, isn't it,' Soloman said. 'It's not definite is it?'

'Seems quite probable though,' Jeffers replied. 'There's nothing else at present!'

Soloman thought back to his last big case. There had been only a few leads with that missing trousered leg. Patience and perseverance had worked in the end and they had managed to come to a positive outcome.

They made their way off the main roads and into the city of Brighton. The satnav took them to an industrial area on the northern outskirts. By day it would be busy but now, as darkness slowly took over from dusk, the low buildings stood silently side by side. There was little movement, only the last of the late workers leaving.

They turned into a dead end street and there at the end was one illuminated sign.

Chapter 19

The Monkey Bar sign was not bright. It was a poor excuse for advertising the club but perhaps that was the idea. After all, this building would be open when everything else in the street would be closed. Some rather pathetic LED rope lighting did little to welcome guests or those that had never been before who needed some encouragement. It was far from being a salubrious area and Soloman and Jeffers both wondered what they were going to find inside.

There were three cars parked outside. Jeffers drew up alongside the left hand one and applied the brake.

'Here we are then, better find the manager and search through the club database,' Jeffers said, summarising their recent thoughts. They rang the bell, aware that they were being watched by the CCTV camera overhead.

'These clubs can be a bit suspicious, so I understand, about letting single blokes in, so perhaps we had better hold up our warrant cards, as there are two of us.' They both held up their cards and then there was a crackle as the door intercom came to life.

'What can we do for you?' a rather blunt female voice came out of the box on the wall.

'Police here,' Soloman said, still holding up his card. 'We need to speak with you, can you open the door please?'

Eventually, the big black door opened and a smartly dressed woman in designer business wear stood on the other side of the threshold. It was not what Soloman and Jeffers were expecting, as her apparel was more appropriate for meeting wealthy clients, to secure some advantageous deal.

Perhaps by day she is Chief Executive Officer of some big company, Soloman thought but his thoughts were interrupted.

'What's the problem then?' the woman abruptly asked.

'We need to interrogate your member database,' Jeffers began.

'I'm afraid it's completely confidential. When signing up for membership all of our guests are given a one hundred percent assurance that their details will be kept confidentially.'

The woman stood her ground, as if she was used to this sort of confrontation on the doorstep.

'There's a link between two of your members and one of our very serious, ongoing cases. Would you prefer if we came back with a full search warrant and a team of police, which would be far more invasive to all your clients, than if we just come in now, find out what we need to know and then leave? We know what goes on here. That really is not our concern but a serious crime is and that is why we need your help. It's not as if you are busy,' Jeffers said, looking around at the three cars parked outside and having finally finished, he looked at the woman questioningly.

Without further ado, she stood aside to let Soloman and Jeffers in. They both looked around at their surroundings. In front of them was a smart reception desk and two stylish easy chairs. It appeared to both of the policemen that they had entered quite a different world, to the one on the other side of the door. A plush carpet, tasteful artwork, a large mirror and expensive floral arrangements provided an immediate contrast to the rather grubby and industrial area they had left outside.

'Better follow me to my office,' the woman said, having studied their warrant cards.

They all went upstairs and in through an unmarked door. The entrance way and stairs were tastefully lit and the expensive carpet carried on into the woman's smart office.

'Who is it that you are looking for?' the woman said, as she sat down at her computer screen and started tapping in her access codes.

'Just before we begin, we need to make a note of your name,' Soloman said.

'Christine Harper but they all call me Chrissy here,' the woman said, softening slightly, as she began to understand the full implications of what was happening.

'We only have initials and a telephone number for a couple in Worthing. They are 'R and S.''

'Not much to go on then, I hope that we find this couple quickly. Mondays can be surprisingly busy. It is just as well that I have an assistant tonight to work on the reception desk.'

Chrissy accessed the guest file and together they started the rather lengthy process of wading through all five hundred and sixty five members of The Monkey Club. She seemed to have softened completely now. Always best to be helpful to the police, she thought. You never know when you might need them.

They didn't have a surname, so looking for an 'R and S' and then a surname certainly took some time and much patience was needed. Indeed, it could be an 'S and R' so they had to be mindful of that too. After an hour and a half and with no sign of success, Chrissy offered them coffee. She called downstairs and five minutes later one of her colleagues arrived at the door with a cafetiere, three cups and a plate of biscuits. She looked at the two policemen with a certain curiosity.

'It's getting quite busy out there, Chrissy,' she said at the doorway as she turned to leave.

 As she opened the door there was indeed a great deal of noise, coming from the main lounge and bar.

'I can't believe it for a Monday night,' Jeffers said.

As luck would have it they didn't need to go past the H's. There it was, Robert and Sara Hughes, with an address in Worthing. They had been members for six years. According to the records Robert was forty two whilst Sara was forty one.

'If we are quick, we can visit them this evening. Worthing is not too far from Brighton and the traffic will have eased.' Soloman said, jumping to his feet and gathering his jacket. 'Hopefully we can be there by nine thirty.'

A look of dismay, quickly hidden, crossed Jeffers's face as he realised that it was not Soloman's intention to call it a day and head off for a beer.

'Yes, we must,' he said adding a positive note, as they left the office and made their way down the stairs.

The queue at reception was ten deep and as he was about to go through the door, an idea came to him, what if Robert and Sara were here now? They might even be standing in this queue in front of him.

He returned to Chrissy and together they checked who had signed in that evening. She looked along the queue and confirmed that they were not there.

'I don't think they usually come in on a Monday night,' Chrissy said, 'more of a Saturday couple.'

Having thanked her, the two policemen left the building and walked to their car. The car park was nearly full now. Monday certainly was a popular night.

It was a true summer's evening, as they made their way along the A27 to Worthing. There seemed to be no sign of the heat of the day dissipating. The lack of rain was making everything very dusty and Soloman and Jeffers could both tell that it was going to be another humid night.

The Hughes lived on the far side of Worthing, not far from the seafront. Jeffers was driving and this allowed Soloman to take in his surroundings and look at the scenery. It was all part of his police training and this was an area that he was particularly good at. He was genuinely interested in people and his forte was noticing how they lived. He could quickly scan a room and remember all the details. It was the same outside in a garden or outbuilding.

They turned into the road where the Hughes lived. Solomon immediately noticed that these were all semi-detached properties built in the 1950s. They would probably be reasonably large by current standards and they would all follow the same design. Some would have extensions at the back, or in the attic. Some would have fabulous gardens, cramming marvellous horticulture into a small space.

They pulled up outside number thirty eight. Soloman was slightly disappointed. A plain exterior greeted him with a square lawn in front and a tarmac drive to one side. A silver Ford Focus car was parked there. The otherwise immaculate lawn was the only positive thing in this dreary frontage. There were no shrubs or plants and the front boundary was marked with a low brick wall. A pair of wooden gates stood permanently open.

Soloman and Jeffers rang the bell and braced themselves for whatever was to happen next. It was nine forty eight and late in the day to be standing uninvited on someone's doorstep.

The front door was cautiously opened on the security chain.

'Good evening,' Soloman began. He and Jeffers held up their warrant cards, 'I am DC Soloman and this is DS Jeffers. We are from the Devon and Cornwall constabulary. I am sorry to be calling so late but we need to speak with you urgently, may we come inside?'

The figure inside was a short woman who looked up at the policemen.

'It's not my son Jamie is it?' she said, her motherly instinct kicking in.

'No, it's nothing to do with your family. It is you and your husband that we need to speak with.

'Who is it Sara?' a man's voice spoke from somewhere inside.

'It's the police,' the woman in front of Soloman and Jeffers said, turning her head to speak over her shoulder, 'wanting to speak with us.'

'Better let them in,' the male voice continued, the owner appearing at his wife's side.

The security chain was slide back and the door opened.

'You had better come in,'

Soloman and Jeffers stepped over the threshold onto a dark beige carpet and into a beige hallway. The stairs traditionally rose to the left and the same beige carpet ascended upwards.

'You are Sara and Robert Hughes?' Soloman said questioningly.

'Yes.' they both said together rather cautiously, fearful that they were incriminating themselves.

Sara was wearing a pink dressing gown and Robert still wore brown work trousers and a cream shirt. He was considerably taller than his wife with a traditional 'short back and sides' haircut and slightly greying sideburns. They appeared a very ordinary couple but one that was closely united as he lent over Sara's shoulder.

He gestured towards the lounge door and they all in turn gathered in another beige room. A large television dominated a corner next to the fireplace and his-and-her chairs were positioned in front of the big screen.

'What's all this about?' Robert asked, now standing in front of his chair. The room was not overly large and at this point Soloman and Jeffers took it upon themselves to sit down on the sofa under the front window which faced the two chairs.

'Your initials have appeared on the computer of a couple who have gone missing.' Soloman began, not wishing to waste any more time. 'What can you tell us about your associations with Chris and Bridget Tamworth?' A direct question was what was needed now, Soloman had decided.

A rather lengthy pause followed, while the enormity of the question sunk in. Robert wondered what it was exactly that they were being asked and more to the point, how much did the police know? At last he spoke.

'We met the Tamworths socially last year. They are a very pleasant couple and we had similar interests, but we only met them once.'

'You are quite sure about meeting them just the once?' Jeffers repeated the statement.

'Yes, it was last June, the last weekend just before my birthday. I remember it well.' Robert spoke up, whilst Sara, who was unsure of the situation, stood behind her husband.

Her confidence having returned, she stepped forward and faced Jeffers and Soloman, 'I really don't understand why there is an inference that we might be involved with the disappearance of this couple.'

It was a statement rather than a question and Sara's voice had grown stronger. It did not warrant an answer, Solomon decided.

'So, I need to ask you both, where were you the week before last?'

Robert and Sara looked visibly shaken by the directness.

'You were away on that course, weren't you?' Sara said turning to Robert. There was surety in her voice and her tone was forthright. Did she have something to hide, Soloman wondered. 'I am a dental nurse during the day and in the evening I visit my mother. She is looked after during the day by her next door neighbour but in the evening, I take over. Although now very frail, she is fiercely independent. I always call in at the neighbour first to see how the day has gone. Both she and Mum would be able to vouch for me. Robert works for the local garden centre. They are part of a chain and that week he was away training at another branch in Manchester. It would therefore be impossible for either of us to be involved in the disappearance of the Tamworths in Cornwall.'

By the end, Sara had completely rallied and the previous shy, retiring and rather demure person had disappeared.

'That is all very useful, thank you. Give us the relevant names of the people who can vouch for you.' Soloman had softened his voice.

Robert went to a desk in the corner and started writing down the names, addresses and telephone numbers. While this was happening, Soloman went on a tour of the house. He was not sure what he was looking for, but his police training told him that he would notice anything that was out of place and not as it should be.

The beige theme continued throughout the first floor, which was made up of two reasonable bedrooms, a box room and a bathroom. It was all very plain; some would say a little dated and uninspiring. Everything had a feeling that it was past its sell-by date, slightly worn and unloved.

As Soloman looked out of the back bedroom window and into the garden below, he could see another immaculate lawn with neatly trimmed edges and thick green grass. It was completely square with a concrete surround, just wide enough to walk on, presumably to tend the edges. The garden was floodlit by security lighting from the yard of the lock-up business that butted onto the back boundary.

By this light, Soloman could clearly see the back of the garage and a wooden garden shed. It was not a big garden, only twenty foot square at maximum. Not a single shrub, tree, or flower adorned this place. Soloman was quite intrigued by the starkness and the lack of thought behind it. He wondered, why, when one could do so much with a small space.

He retraced his steps back downstairs over the beige carpet and cream painted walls. He entered the small kitchen at the back of the house. It was fully fitted, with dark oak cupboards; this little space adding to the dismal feeling that the house radiated.

Dirty plates and saucepans covered the work surfaces by the sink, presumably from the Hughes' supper. A little window was positioned next to the back door.

Soloman returned to the hall and looked around the door of the dining room. A pair of French doors overlooked the same small back garden. The curtains were not drawn and the garden was as light as day thanks to the floodlighting from the yard behind.

'I need to look in the garage and shed.' Soloman said. 'Do I need a key?'

'They are on a set in the back door lock.' Sara said. She sounded tired.

Soloman was surprised that he had not been questioned over his desire to see outside. He left the confines of the stuffy house and was grateful for the comparatively fresh air even though it was still warm.

The garage was tidy with everything in its place and the floor was clean. The lawn mower looked new, almost polished. The shed was the same. Neither place had accumulated piles of unwanted objects and so feeling slightly disappointed that there was nothing there to help the case, Soloman locked up and returned inside.

He found the others in the lounge. They turned to face him as he entered and spoke, 'That will be all for now. Thank you for your time and we are sorry to have disturbed you so late.' It was ten thirty.

'Where does this leave us now?' Robert said. There was a slightly aggressive tone in his voice.

'We will let you know if we need you any further. As long as this all checks out satisfactorily, we won't need to speak with you again.' Soloman waved the piece of paper containing the names and addresses.

Soloman and Jeffers climbed into the car and drove off into the night to their Travelodge. It was only a short journey but just as they were parking, Soloman's phone rang. It was Jessica.

113

Soloman spoke first, 'You're working late, everything ok?'

'We think that you should check out the Goldilocks club in Portsmouth. It looks like there is every chance that the other couple might be members. Hopefully you can get an address from them. It would in any case be a good place to start. Let me know if there is anything else we can do.'

Jeffers relayed the possible alibis that Robert and Sara Hughes had given them. 'Check these details out tomorrow. We will see if the Hughes' are as squeaky clean as they make out. Well done but get some rest now.'

The call was ended and Soloman and Jeffers sat in the car pondering over what was now clearly going to be tomorrow's work.

'We will discuss this over breakfast. It is too late now,' Soloman said at last. 'We may not have found out anything new today but we have another chance tomorrow.'

Soloman liked working with Jeffers. He was easier to read than Freeman, less emphatic and worked at a more even pace. They both seemed to have a more positive outlook, whereas Freeman, although their boss, could at times find himself in a more depressed state. He usually managed to free himself and the upbeat intensity resumed.

Soloman and Jeffers climbed out of the car and made their way to reception. There was no one present. Jeffers rang the bell and they both leaned on the desk, exhausted by their long day. Eventually a spotty young man appeared. He had a wide smile. Although wearing the regulation business work wear, he did not present a smart image. He was slim and only of average height but somehow looked dishevelled.

'Yes mate,' he said, 'if you are after a room, we are full.'

'We have a reservation.' Soloman said, believing that this would sort out the situation.

'Our computer system crashed this afternoon. Sorry, there is nothing I can do. I am sending everyone to The Portside. They had spaces this afternoon.'

His words were final and he seemed not to care. Soloman was on the point of starting to complain but Jeffers spoke first.

'It's no use arguing here, we will write. What is the number for The Portside?'

Without speaking, the receptionist scribbled the number down on the back of a business card and pushed it forward towards Jeffers. He stood there with his hands in his pockets. He had blond hair cut in an offset and fashionable manner. Soloman noticed a snake tattoo spiralling out of his shirt collar. He wondered idly where it started.

Thankfully, The Portside had one last twin room, and the customer service seemed a little more focused. Soloman and Jeffers climbed wearily back into the car and drove the three miles.

The Portside was a large double-fronted hotel overlooking the old port section of the city near the waterfront. It was painted a pleasant blue. Soloman and Jeffers walked in via a conservatory entrance. There was a pleasant ambiance and soft gentle music playing in the background. The cool grey painted walls and white woodwork gave an upmarket feel and Soloman and Jeffers began to relax.

They checked in and Soloman hung back while Jeffers made his way to the room. Standing in the hallway he made a brief good night call to Richard. All was well in Bristol and Richard was pleased to have a chat.

Ten minutes later, Soloman was having a brief recap on the day's events, with Jeffers whom he found lying on his bed looking exhausted. Soon after they both fell asleep.

Chapter 20

Soloman and Jeffers slept well. After a delicious full English breakfast, on which The Portside prided itself, they left and set off for the Goldilocks Club.

They were close to the main road and soon found themselves nearing the outskirts of Portsmouth. Ten minutes later, having followed the satnav directions, they found themselves driving down a quiet lane. Behind the trees which lined the road, there were large houses set well back. They had extensive and manicured lawns, neatly clipped shrubs and well-tended flower beds. This was a smart suburb on the outskirts of the city. Soloman took it all in. At the bottom of this road, which gradually descended, they were met with a large gate, tall and forbidding. On either side of the sturdy gate posts, trees and bushes created a thick screen. It was impossible to see what was on the other side.

A polite notice, on the gate asked guests to ring the bell at the side. There was no indication that this was The Goldilocks Club.

Soloman pressed the intercom button and their call was eventually answered.

'Yes,' the male voice said.

'Is this the Goldilocks Club?' Soloman asked.

'Who's wanting to know?' the reply came back.

'DC Soloman and DS Jeffers,' Soloman responded.

There was a moment's pause and then the disembodied voice asked, 'What's it about?'

'Can you let us in and then we can explain?'

There was another pause and the sound of muffled voices in the background, decisions were being made as to whether these two policemen were going to be let in.

Soloman spoke again, 'That was a polite request, but not something that can be declined. We are here on urgent police business and at the moment you are obstructing our lines of enquiry.'

'I'm on my way,' a rather meek reply came back immediately.

Soloman and Jeffers found their identity cards and waited patiently. After another five minutes the gate was slowly opened and a rather breathless man in his early fifties stood the other side. He peered at the identification, not sure of what he was actually looking at.

Soloman and Jeffers found themselves looking into a Garden of Eden. This setup was totally different to The Monkey Bar in the industrial area.

A sweeping lawn led down to a rustic wood cabin which was next to a big old barn both of which were in a good state of repair. Mature shrubs and enclosed sitting areas provided shelter from any wind. In the distance a stream flowed through this paradise. On the other side was a copse reached by an old wooden pedestrian bridge.

Soloman and Jeffers looked from one side to the other.

'Not sure what I was expecting but it wasn't this,' Jeffers said at last.

'Me neither,' was all Soloman could muster, his eyes wide open in amazement.

'Anyway, back to business,' Jeffers said. 'This is The Goldilocks Club?'

A nod acted as confirmation.

'We need to see your current membership list. We are looking for two persons who may be connected with a current criminal investigation.'

'I'm only the cleaner,' the other man said. 'You had better come inside and meet the boss. You're lucky he is here this morning. It's usually just me on a Tuesday morning.'

Together they moved down the path to the wooden cabin reception room.

'Pete, two policemen here to see you,' he said, speaking towards a back office, once they were inside.

A man slightly younger than either Soloman or Jeffers were expecting, walked into the front reception area. It was a wonderfully sunny room with comfortable conservatory-style sofas and chairs. A glass topped table acted as a reception desk and on one side a large vase stood filled with an abundance of freshly cut sweet peas which gave off a sweet fragrance. It was relaxing and welcoming.

Pete looked at the policemen enquiringly.

Soloman repeated their request to look at the database. Eventually, Pete succumbed and both detectives settled themselves down at the computer, looking for a D and an H. After three hours of intensive scrutiny, they came across a Dominic and Heather Wilkins. Taking the address, Soloman and Jeffers left The Goldilocks Club and again followed the directions.

Chapter 21

It was a slightly cooler and more overcast day. The satnav said that the journey was five miles and when they began to draw nearer to the address, they found themselves entering a small village. It had a run down and tired appearance. They passed a small convenience store with its windows covered in posters describing this week's special offers. The overflowing rubbish bin outside did little to inspire one to the area.

Soloman had guessed by the address that they would be visiting a park home estate. He found that he was correct as Jeffers turned left through the entrance into the narrow side road.

It was an established and neat estate with a mixture of bungalows. Number forty five was of the older variety. The front garden was bordered with a low hedge and a small red hatchback was parked in one of the two parking spaces adjacent to the end of the building.

It was now approaching lunchtime, as Soloman and Jeffers stood on the front door- step with their identity cards in hand. The door was cautiously opened on the security chain and a petite and nervous woman wearing glasses peered through the opening. She was in her seventies but looked somewhat older, despite her dyed hair which was now a very dark glossy black. She didn't speak so Jeffers started the conversation.

'Good afternoon, this is DC Soloman and I am DS Jeffers.' Warrant cards were held up and the woman recoiled slightly as they were pushed in her direction. 'We are looking for Dominic and Heather Wilkins. Are they at home?'

Jeffers had already decided not to give this woman a choice in the matter as to whether they lived there or not. Assumption was sometimes the best policy. They knew they were correct and it would save time. It paid off.

'They are not here. They have gone away.'

She was just about to close the door but Jeffers was too quick for her and placed his size ten booted foot in the doorway.

'I don't mean to be rude.' he continued, 'but we need to come in and chat with you. It's very important.'

'I'm not keen,' but seeing the large boot in her doorway, she continued, 'alright, I'll just take the chain off.'

The door was closed, chain removed and Jeffers and Soloman stepped inside. There seemed to be a multitude of doors and it was a tight fit with the three of them squeezed into the small hallway.

'You had better follow me.'

They followed her down the passageway which was made even narrower by a large dark and heavy sideboard. They arrived in a small square sitting room. It overlooked a pretty garden, in the middle of which was a small pond with a twinkling fountain. Most of one wall was dominated by a large television. A game show was noisily showing and Soloman pointedly looked at it.

'Mind if we sit down and the television is switched off?'

121

The woman gestured to the green Dralon-covered armchairs and reluctantly fumbled with a remote control until the television became silent.

'Dominic and Heather Wilkins live here but are away at present on holiday? Is that what you are telling us?'

Realising that she had no option but to answer, the woman replied, 'my son and his wife live here with me. That is correct. They are camping in the Lake District. Why do you want to know?'

'We need to speak with them in connection with an ongoing line of inquiry. Their names have come up and we need to clear them, so that we can proceed. Do you have a mobile number for them?' Soloman paused briefly, 'do you know exactly where they are?'

The woman reached for her handbag that was down the side of the sofa. She eventually found the number and having written it down, she handed it to Jeffers.

'I rang my son last night. He said that they were having a great time and were near Lake Windermere. The weather is good up there, just like here.' She smiled as if pleased that they were having a good holiday.

Soloman and Jeffers were not bothered with the intricacies of her son's holiday and instead, Jeffers asked to be shown their bedroom as he wished to view it.

The woman rose and seemed more compliant now. He was taken to the second door on the left and entered a tiny double bedroom. When she returned to Soloman in the sitting room, he asked her when her son had left for the Lake District.

'Three weeks last Saturday,' she replied, 'they haven't had a holiday in five years and he is now between jobs. He thought he would take the opportunity for a decent break.'

Soloman made notes and then he spoke again, 'I'll just have a look around too.'

With that, he entered the kitchen, bathroom and the only other bedroom. There was nothing untoward in any of these rooms. All were very small with overly large pieces of heavy furniture, perhaps from a previous life and home. They were not suitable being placed wherever there was a space. The living room and the bedrooms had ticking clocks. Time passed slowly here.

He joined Jeffers in the second bedroom. A small double bed filled the room. Along one side were a set of fitted wardrobes. Jeffers had already been through these and was now staring at a laptop.

'We had better take this. Write out a receipt for it.'

'Have you been through these drawers?' Soloman asked.

'Not yet.'

Soloman started searching through the extensive drawers below the dressing table mirror. However, there was nothing noteworthy there.

They left a slightly bewildered Mrs Wilkins on the doorstep. It had all happened in a flash. She peered up and down the road to see if any of her neighbours had seen her saying goodbye to two men that lunchtime. Betty, who lived two houses down the street, was pretending to be putting something in the rubbish bin. As Soloman and Jeffers drove off, she waved frantically at Dorothy.

'Everything alright?'

'Yes, ta love,' Dorothy closed the front door behind her.

'Better get this analysed as soon as possible. Hopefully there will be some leads.' Soloman said.

It was grey and overcast, but there was still heat in the humid air.

Soloman and Jeffers drove directly to the police headquarters in Portsmouth and handed the laptop over to the relevant department. They were assigned a desk and straight away telephoned Dominic Wilkins who answered after the tenth ring. He and Heather had been walking that morning and were now having a late pub lunch. He confirmed his name and after the situation had been explained, he reluctantly agreed to visit the nearest police station with some identification and proof of being in the Lake District area.

Jeffers informed the nearest police station and the team there promised to make their checks completely watertight.

Soloman and Jeffers sat at the desk. Jeffers idly twiddled his pen between his thumb and forefinger and gazed into open space. Soloman had seen him do this before and knew that he was deep in thought. They drank several cups of coffee and telephoned the Bodmin headquarters to see if there were any further leads that needed checking out in the South East, but there weren't. All had gone quiet.

As there was nothing further to do in the area, both decided to drive back to Cornwall. They stepped out of the air-conditioned building and were met with considerable heat. Despite being grey and overcast, the temperature and humidity had risen during the afternoon.

'Might be in for a thunderstorm, by the look of those clouds,' Jeffers said as he reversed out of the parking space.

'Although I'm from Reading, I shall be glad to get back to the South West. I can't take all this traffic and fumes. There is no fresh air here either.'

'A quieter pace of life,' Jeffers summarised and their journey continued.

Soloman slept for part of the journey and was amazed to find that they were passing Launceston on the main road a few hours later. They did not reach Bodmin until eight o'clock.

Jeffers dropped Soloman off outside the entrance to his flat and proceeded to his own home. Soloman stumbled up to the second floor and made his way into the kitchen. Despite his snooze on the way home, he was feeling tired and deflated. Another twenty four hours had passed. Two further leads had been addressed but it looked as though they were not going to lead anywhere.

He made himself his favourite snack, cheese on toast. There wasn't much in the cupboard or fridge. He had been so busy deputising for Freeman and in effect doing the work of two persons that he had not given much thought to a grocery shop. Having eaten, he decided that although it was still relatively early, he would catch up on some sleep. It was good to be back in his own bed. But first he must ring Richard. Texting was all very well but it was much better to hear a real voice. Richard was out running, very pleased to hear Ore's voice and wanted to hear all about his day. He promised to call him back when he was home.

Ore went to brush his teeth and had just climbed into bed when his phone rang. He reached for it and laid his head on the pillow. It was a good way to end what had been two hectic days.

Chapter 22

Gavin Freeman woke early the following morning to a bright Wednesday. As he lay there, he realised that they were being blessed with a truly lovely summer. He felt happy. His wife and new baby were doing well; his mother was much better and had agreed to help that day with the household. Gavin could therefore go into work and catch up on the case.

He sat down at his desk at ten minutes past eight. He had collected a large black coffee from the machine in the corner and began to read his emails.

'Glad to see you back,' a cheery voice said across the open plan office as Superintendent Marshall made her way across the floor to her office in the corner.

'Come to my office when Soloman and Jeffers arrive. We need to have a catch-up. How are mother and baby doing?' The latter was almost an afterthought.

'Will do, thanks and yes, all good at home.'

'I'm so pleased,' she smiled, 'and we really need to get this case sorted.' The smile changed to a knowing look as she entered her office.

Jeffers arrived next, looking tired, unlike Soloman ten minutes later who seemed refreshed.

'Two emails have just come through that are very relevant amidst all the others that I have got to wade through,' Freeman said as Jeffers and Soloman as they made their way towards their desks.

'Gather round and then Marshall wants us.'

The first email was from the Windermere constabulary reporting that at eight thirty last night Dominic and Heather Wilkins had arrived at the station to identify themselves. They had both produced driving licences and most importantly a receipt from the campsite, where they were staying, showing that they had paid in cash just over three weeks before, when they had arrived. They had a plethora of other receipts, petrol, supermarkets, several pub meals, a cinema visit, a fishing trip on a boat on Lake Windermere and several clothing receipts. These all evidenced that they had been in the Lake District during the time that they had said.

The warden at the campsite had been contacted by the police and he had checked his CCTV at the barriers and confirmed that the Wilkins had consistently left and entered the site, sometimes several times a day. They had also had a newspaper on order at the on-site shop, which they had dutifully collected each morning at the same time.

At that moment Jessica appeared, 'the alibis of Robert and Sara Hughes' all check out. They were where they said they were and at the times stated,' She smiled briefly as if congratulating herself on her news. She was met with a wall of solemn faces rigid in their expression.

'Looks like they can be eliminated from our enquiries,' Jeffers said at last when the three of them had digested this new information.

'What a complete nuisance and waste of time that all was,' Soloman added, 'I really thought we might be getting somewhere.'

'Wait a minute,' Freeman said, 'the other email is from the Portsmouth police, about the laptop.'

They all peered at the screen.

'There is nothing there either,' Soloman said a moment later.

'That is correct,' Freeman responded, as he finished reading the last sentence, 'it seems that the team have found a few risqué photos, but nothing illegal. The team did scrutinise the calendar and whilst there wasn't much on it, they did find reference to meetings with the Tamworths over two weekends last August.'

'That all seems to fit,' Jeffers said, 'but it doesn't lead us anywhere. The Superintendent is not going to be very pleased. We had better get over to her office.'

The three of them made their way across the floor, refilling their coffee mugs as they passed the coffee machine. They opened the glass door and rather sheepishly walked in. Louise Marshall could tell by their stance and demeanour that they did not have any positive news for her. They collectively brought her up to date, giving full details of the trip to the Goldilocks Club and the Monkey Bar. Soloman and Jeffers explained about their meetings with the Hughes and the Wilkins' mother. When they had finished, there was silence in the room, as they all digested these thoughts.

'We have no more leads then?' Marshall finally spoke, 'everything is a blank?'

They all nodded.

'We will keep the dedicated telephone lines open but reduce them and the number of operators down to one. Any queries or leads we will follow up immediately. I have no option now but to downgrade this operation, as sad as this case is and as sorry as I am for Simon and Vanessa Tamworth. We do have other work to attend to but if anything comes to light we will immediately prioritise it.'

Crestfallen glances passed around the room. Soloman felt particularly sad as it was he who had personally spoken to Simon and as a result he felt that he had made a personal connection with him. They left the office. Soloman suggested that he himself should telephone Simon and give him the news. He sat at his desk letting differing thoughts pass through his mind while he formulated how he was going to impart this news.

He picked up the receiver and dialled the number for the Chichester Leisure Centre. The call was answered and he was put on hold while Simon was sought and tannoyed to come to the phone. He imagined what he would be thinking as he made his way to the manager's office. Would it be good news or not so good? Have they found my parents or not?

'Simon Tamworth here, what news have you got? He sounded upbeat and hopeful.

'DC Soloman here from the Cornwall Police, this is just an update but I am sorry, I don't have any news for you,' he paused.

'Oh, I thought.......' Simon's voice trailed off. Something, anything would be better than this empty nothing.

The upbeat and positive tone had dissipated, like a sharply pricked balloon.

'We did have some new leads which we have followed up, both in Worthing and Portsmouth but neither of these are going forward. We will be keeping the dedicated telephone lines open and follow up immediately on anything that comes to light. How are you both doing?'

'We are coping but only just. Vanessa has gone moody and I am struggling to get my head around it all. It seems so strange for them not to be here, especially after we had all been so happy having just moved into Mum and Dad's dream house.'

'I'll make sure that the police liaison officer checks on you every day and updates you. Is that okay and can we do anything further for you Simon?'

There wasn't anything else anyone could do, not until they were found, either dead or alive.

Soloman felt completely deflated. It was as if someone had punched him in the stomach. What on earth must it be like for Simon and Vanessa? He thought.

Chapter 23

Harry Winds had been a farmer all his life. He had been fortunate enough to be the only son and heir and had inherited the farm on the south side of Bodmin from his father, who in turn had inherited it from his father. The farm had been in the same family for three hundred years.

Over those years there had been many changes. Some had seen good times and others, much leaner. The two world wars had been a real challenge in their time. There had been a lack of manpower and although willing, many of the extra helpers had not known the first thing about farming. Their determination, enthusiasm and hard work had seen them through those difficult times and the farm had survived. Some of the subsequent generations had been good, whilst others had been lazy and had used the reserves of money and stock.

The name of Winds was well known locally and generally it was held in good stead, especially if the family at the time had been good employers and helpers in the community around about. It was a large farm, which somehow had survived being divided up in the leaner years by the greedier inheritors. As a result, the family were at times put on the pedestal of landed gentry. Most were hard workers and good employers but that didn't stop any gossip being spread in the local pubs and shops.

The farmhouse was a grand building facing south and built on the side of a hill. The land stretching behind and in front belonged to the farm. To one side there was an extensive collection of farm buildings, which had been built over the years. Some were in a better state of repair than others. In front there was a long drive leading down to the lane.

Harry Winds had let the farm run down. He still had his dairy herd and a daily milk collection but he was a lazy man, who didn't like work or commitment. He left most of the day to day running of the household and farm to his long suffering wife. Anna was a petite woman, a few years younger than her husband who was in his mid-fifties. What she lost in stature, she more than made up for in energy. She and Harry had two sons, Edward and Howard. Edward was twenty-five and Howard was twenty-three. They had inherited their father's tendency to laziness and only worked when it was needed. Both were tall and broad-shouldered men with a liking for beer and a dislike of authority. The only person that they seemed to respect was their mother. She had somehow managed to instil the need for better behaviour when she spoke.

Harry and his sons would much rather spend the afternoon and evening in the local pub, rather than keep on top of any maintenance, repairs or improvements. As a result, the once grand facade to the farmhouse had faded. Windows were now rotten and paint free. The roof leaked in several places and the walls had turned green in the damp Cornish air. The concrete drive that had been replaced in the 1970s at great expense was now badly cracked and disintegrating. It was the same story with the barns and machinery. Any repairs that were done were carried out by the cheapest method. Harry Winds was known locally as Mr Skinflint and even his old Land Rover had seen better days.

As far as Harry was concerned, his sons had complete run of the place but in their eyes, this meant wasting time on their mobile phones. Work was something that had to be done but only as a last resort.

There was no sign of stability in any of the relationships that either son had with any of the local girls. There had been several near misses as far as pregnancies were concerned and several times cross words had nearly got out of hand in the local pub between Harry and various fathers in the locality.

It was now late September and it had been a fabulous summer. The correct amount of rain and sunshine had produced a plentiful supply of rich grass and the milk yields had been excellent. Clotted cream had been in great demand, with the high level of visitors to the South West and all round profits were good.

On the last Sunday of September, Harry Winds' goddaughter, Rachel, was having her new baby christened. She was the daughter of Harry's best and old friend Thomas, who ran a successful garage and car repair centre in Liskeard. It was to be a big two-family celebration and Edward Winds had been asked to be a godfather.

As it had been such a wonderful summer, Anna Winds had felt confident that the weather would hold and had arranged for a marquee and a big party after the church service.

The preparations had all gone well that weekend. The marquee had been erected on the Saturday and the caterers had duly arrived on the Sunday morning. Luckily they had arrived just before the service and Anna had managed to organise them in her usual efficient manner. The sun was shining and the early morning dew was evaporating in the warmth. The birds were singing and the garden looked a picture. She had worked hard on this and the roses were still flowering.

But unsurprisingly, her boys had let her down. Clean ironed shirts and ties had been laid out on their beds after breakfast and new suits had been purchased for this smart event in their calendar.

However, half an hour before the church service was due to start, there was no sign of them.

Harry, in his usual style, was not unduly worried. As long as he could get to the pub afterwards and before he was expected back at the house for the big lunch, he wasn't worried.

At the last minute, just when the vicar was calling for the godparents to come forward to the font, Edward and Howard appeared, breathless and with ties askew. No comments were made and the rest of the service and the christening passed without issue.

The congregation were in good spirits, as they emerged from the dark interior of the cool church, into the bright midday sun. The guests made their way slowly in dribs and drabs back to the farm and Harry, who had visited the pub for a quick pint, had returned eventually with his two sons. The caterers had done an excellent job and soon lunch was underway.

Fifteen years earlier, Howard Winds, at the age of eight, had been diagnosed as being on the autistic spectrum. Close friends and family understood his situation. Generally, his autism manifested itself in speaking about things at inappropriate moments. But one thing that everyone knew, was that he was incapable of lying. Just after the main course had been served, Anna spoke to Howard in the seat beside her.

'Everything alright Howard, you were late at the service?' It was a question and a statement in one.

'Yes Mum, me and Edward were out on the quads. Hadn't been down to the "bottom" field in ages, thought we would. There was a mangled car tipped over the edge in the pit. Looked like there had been a fire. Must have been bad, no paint, going rusty. That's why we were late.'

Anna turned to Edward.

'Do you know how long it's been there?'

'No, haven't been down there since May when we mended the fence. We don't need to go now that the cows don't get out anymore. We only climbed over the fence because Howard wanted to and you know how he is when he has a fixed idea.'

She turned to Harry.

'Not now Anna,' he said, knowing the look he was receiving and not wanting to be quizzed in front of his friends.

It wasn't until the following day, that Anna, who had had a sleepless night worrying about it, decided that enough was enough. The police should know about this car and they could take it from there. They couldn't just leave it; it must have belonged to someone.

Perhaps it was stolen and never found. It all seemed a bit odd to Anna. Why would a car be dumped on their land if there wasn't something at least a little bit suspicious? It seemed to her and she was very much a thinking person, that something wasn't right. What if the car had been put in the pit to hide it and why was it so badly burnt? It was a mile from the house and access from the nearest lane was through a five bar gate, up a short track amidst quite dense trees and then a short way across the bottom of the field to where the little pit was. The pit was surrounded by trees and because of the danger that it posed to cattle, a fence had been placed around part of it and this became the new boundary. From here the field rose up. The pit was effectively in no man's land as far as being discovered and there was no reason to venture into this part.

Chapter 24

Anna's call to the Bodmin Police Station was recorded as being at fifteen minutes past ten on the following Monday morning.

Freeman, Soloman and Jeffers were informed of the remains of the dumped car, whilst sitting around Freeman's desk, discussing another current case.

Mrs Winds had categorically stated on the telephone that someone had gone to great lengths to conceal this abandoned car. What else were they concealing? This was not a burnt out joy riders dream, or a tight hairpin bend that an inexperienced driver had taken too quickly. No this had been meticulously planned.

Freeman and his team had been summoned to join the rescue team, just in case there really was more to this. The three of them travelled in Freeman's car and waited for the recovery truck, complete with lifting gear to arrive. Normally a damaged vehicle would be left to the insurance company or the land-owner to deal with but in this instance, because of the possible suspicious circumstances, the recovery team had been called.

Freeman, Soloman and Jeffers found the five bar gate, which they opened and walked up to the pit. It was about sixty feet wide and twenty deep. It had been created by a stray bomb, from a German aircraft, releasing its remaining load before returning home during the Second World War.

The surrounding trees created a dark and slightly foreboding atmosphere, after the bright sun of that early autumn day. Occasionally a car passed in the lane.

There, before them, just as Mrs Winds had stated was the crumpled remains of a medium-sized car. It was lying on its side.

'Looks like it has been pushed over the edge,' Jeffers said, breaking the silence but expressing the obvious, as they looked on at the devastating scene.

'Been a fire too,' Soloman said. 'I wonder what colour it was, must have been allowed to burn out, no sign of being extinguished. Must have been intense but perhaps not much fuel in the tank, as there doesn't appear to have been an explosion. Only the VIN to help us identify it.'

'Check with the fire brigade,' Freeman added, turning to Jeffers and looking around at the trees and bushes, 'just to make absolutely sure that they were never called to this spot.'

It really was the perfect place to hide a car fire, self-contained, down in a pit, miles from any houses and with only a quiet lane nearby. There might just have been a plume of smoke. In daylight, this would have looked like a farm bonfire. If at night, no one would have been any the wiser.

'Chase up forensics, Soloman please. They need to check this area thoroughly.' Freeman barked. At that moment the sound of a large lorry could be heard. 'If that is the recovery truck, tell them they will have to wait until forensics have done their stuff. We will come back later,' Freeman said 'but first, Soloman, you and I will go up to the house and interview the family. Jeffers, you go back to the station and run the vehicle identification number through the computer. Come back to me immediately with your findings, then I can decide whether we need to investigate further.'

Fifteen minutes later, Freeman and Soloman were standing on the farmhouse doorstep. They started their interviews with Anna, who seemed competent and resolute in her understanding of the seriousness of the situation.

'You called us this morning after your sons found this damaged vehicle on your land yesterday. What else can you tell us?'

'There isn't anything else,' Anna said rather desperately, wishing she could be more helpful. 'I went to look for myself this morning and was horrified by what I saw. Then I came back and reported it.' Secretly she felt very guilty that the car had not been found sooner.

Anna was irritated to the point of frustration that her husband and sons, who together did the outside work with occasional extra help, had been so lax that this car had lain dormant for so many weeks. After all, she looked after the house, did all the farm admin and cooked meals for four, three times a day. She tried to reason with herself that there wasn't actually any need for anyone to have visited this part of their land. The herd had all been safe when they had been grazing in that field.

Then she had another thought. The person or persons who had put the car in their pit, must have been aware that there was a strong likelihood that the car would not be found. It would seem that that was the requirement. Someone had been very clever.

Chapter 25

Howard Winds was the next to be interviewed. Freeman and Soloman were sat in the drawing room of the old farmhouse. Small windows looked south down towards Liskeard, across the lawns, then a field or two and then a bank of trees where the lane ran. The room had faded grandeur. Everything needed an extensive renovation from the oak panelling and floorboards to the heavy tapestry curtains and sofa coverings. Once upon a time these furnishings would have been serviceable but now they were torn and worn through. For the last twenty years, Harry Winds had paid little attention to these finer points. Their three labradors were allowed to come in from a muddy farm-yard and lie on the sofas and chairs. Harry himself and his boys never changed out of their farm clothes. Dirt and detritus lay everywhere.

Anna had long since given up. For the first few years of married life, when they had inherited the farm and with two young sons, she had done her best. Countless toys, ranging in size from train sets to tricycles had been brought in and out. It was their home and all were happy and content amidst the hanging cobwebs and the windows that would now be more likely to fall apart, than be opened.

Now all that Anna was concerned about was whether the kitchen was clean and as none of the men in the house ever entered her world, she managed to fulfil this last desire. At times it was her sanctuary. She even had a small easy chair in one corner of this big room, it was her latest acquisition.

The sun shone brightly, lower in the sky, now that it was the last day of September.

Soloman adjusted his seating position on the sofa and found that he was sitting on half a dog chew. He casually moved a well slobbered rope toy with his right loafer and made a mental note to wear more appropriate footwear, now that most of his work necessitated the need for something more rugged.

Freeman began, 'Howard, how is it that you only found the car yesterday?'

'It's an Auris, one of the later models. I can tell by the rear lights, even though it was all bashed in. I'm right aren't I?'

'Not sure yet, we are running the VIN through the computer. Don't you go down that part of the field very often?'

'No need, mended the fence earlier this year.'

'I see and what did you think when you saw the car?'

'Nothing really, it's just a bashed up car. I like the Auris, where is it now, can I have it?'

'It's in the police yard Howard, do you have anything else to tell us, anything that might tell us who put it there? Did you put it there?'

That question was a last-ditch attempt to surprise a confession from the boys, just in case Howard and his brother had had anything to do with it. It seemed unlikely on reflection as it was he who had told his mother yesterday, or had he just blurted it out by mistake in the wake of the party and the extra family and friends around him?

'No, just found it there, like I said yesterday, before church, made us late.'

'Thank you Howard, that will be all for now but we may wish to speak with you again.'

Having finished the interview Freeman strode the twenty feet to the door and called in Edward. He found him sitting outside the front door, on the veranda, mobile phone in hand.

'We will speak with you now,' his authoritative tone making Edward turn around and look up. Unusually he meekly followed Freeman back into the drawing room and slouched down in his usual place. He half sat and half laid, stretching out his legs in front of him. His whole stance and demeanour was beginning to annoy Freeman, who expected a little more respect. He continued to look at his phone.

'You found this car in the pit at the bottom of the field, yesterday morning. What else can you tell us?' Soloman started.

'Nothing more. It wasn't there when the herd was last in the field which was just after we mended the fence. That was at the beginning of May. We were all over that area then. Bits of fencing, quad bikes etc. No car was there.'

'So, it could have been put there anytime from the start of May to now, and you neither heard nor saw any suspicious behaviour at any time, no one snooping around?'

'That's right, I haven't seen anything.'

Soloman held his gaze for a few seconds, to check that he didn't waver at all. He had an inkling that the young man who was only a year or two younger than himself was telling the truth but he didn't care for his cocky attitude. He had a surety, that came from old money but looking around the room, there wasn't much evidence of wealth there now.

'We may wish to speak with you again,' Soloman concluded.

Freeman and Soloman were just rising to their feet and making their way to the door, when it burst open and Jeffers marched into the room.

'Need to speak with you sir, immediately.' there was an urgency in his tone which made Freeman and Soloman quicken their pace onto the front veranda. They left Edward sloping off towards the kitchen, his nonchalant walk all too evident of his cockiness. 'The car was a blue Auris,' he blurted out unable to control his delight at finding this news.

As soon as the words 'blue Auris' were mentioned, Freeman and Soloman realised that they would be opening up the case again and that the once treasured car belonging to Chris and Bridget Tamworth had been found. At last, they had a breakthrough.

By lunchtime, the area around the pit, trees included, was surrounded by blue and white police incident tape. The forensic duo, Greg and Sue, had arrived dressed in their white coverall suits and were hard at work on their knees. The lane outside the five-barred gate was now filled with police vehicles. It was closed to traffic and an alternative route had been put in place.

By the middle of the afternoon, the local television and radio reporters were stationed at the roadblock desperate for news of what was happening. At first they had no idea that there was the possibility of a connection with the missing persons of the summer.

The first rumours were that there had been a serious car accident in the lane. But when no ambulances had arrived or departed and nothing seemed to be happening, they became frustrated. Some climbed over the barriers in search of a police officer in an effort to find out information, but none was divulged at this stage.

'Greg and Sue are asking for you immediately as there are signs of suspicious activity in the area near the pit,' Jeffers said still trying to find his breath. 'I had no signal down there,' he gesticulated in the direction of the pit, 'it takes too long by car so I ran up.'

They were now walking back at a good pace and out of earshot.

Freeman checked looking over his shoulder, 'what kind of suspicious activity?'

Lowering his voice and bending towards Freeman, he said, 'the possibility of a grave. They are erecting the tent over it now. We all have to put on a coverall and we may be looking at a murder scene.'

They quickened their pace and hurried down the hill. Their thoughts multiplied. What would they find? One or two bodies? How long had they been there? What condition would they be in? Had they been brought to this spot dead or had they been murdered at the side of the pit? Finally, would the bodies turn out to be those of Mr and Mrs Tamworth?

All thoughts of interviewing Harry Winds were put on hold. That would have to be dealt with later.

By the time they had reached the bottom of the field, the scene in front of them had changed. Now completely enclosed by blue and white tape, a constable was standing guard. He handed them the white suits and they hurriedly put them on, before climbing over the wooden railings of the fence.

'Careful sir,' the officer said as Freeman made his way between the bushes. 'There is a pile of soil in front of you, left over presumably from when whoever dug these graves.'

'You sound very positive in your assumptions,' Soloman said.

'Not assumptions, sir, Greg and Sue have just this minute found two bodies in a shallow grave together. The ground would not have been hard to dig, being mainly leaf mould from years of leaf fall.'

Jeffers was walking ahead and then stopped outside the tent. He peered in at the entrance and said, 'it is a bit cramped in there. It looks like the bodies have been here a few weeks.'

'Our suspicions were alerted by the several heaps of ground cover that have recently been tampered with,' Sue confirmed.

Freeman and Soloman peered inside and recoiled in horror at the two disfigured naked bodies that had been uncovered.

'How long have they been there?' Freeman asked having stepped back and talking away from the tent flap.

'Not sure at the moment,' Sue said, 'we will let you know, once we have got this poor pair back to the lab but at this stage, we would say two months or possibly three,' she looked at Greg for confirmation of his agreement.

Freeman, Soloman and Jeffers returned to the edge of the pit and took a few deep breaths.

'Even with all our training, it's still a bit of a shock,' Freeman said looking pale and nauseous.

Soloman had also stepped to one side and was looking ashen. All three gathered their thoughts. It appeared that the very worst tragic event had taken place in what was otherwise a charming spot.

Now shafts of sunlight struck downwards between the trees and bushes and the temperature began to drop. The pit itself was an idyllic spot with smooth sides which had been rounded from years of weathering and covered in dead, dry and fluffy leaves. Here and there were patches of moss and a few blades of grass.

144

'Better get back to the house and interview Harry Winds,' Freeman finally said as they had all recovered.

Chapter 26

Freeman, Soloman and Jeffers left the frenetic police activity and this time drove to the Winds' farmhouse.

'Be good for you to meet all the family,' Freeman said to Jeffers, 'I am not sure what he is like but it might be a good idea if we show a force of strength. It is not every day that two naked bodies are uncovered on your farmland.'

But Harry Winds was not at home. Despite frantic phone calls to his mobile by his wife, he had chosen to ignore her. This was not unusual and he had even paid no attention to her text messages. Anna had stated that he was wanted by the police for interviewing. She had also stated that the dumped car had created a great deal of police interest. But Harry was in his usual place at that time of day and had been all afternoon.

Anna Winds was profusely apologetic to the policemen on her doorstep. Freeman could tell that she was becoming increasingly frustrated by the lack of interest and support from her husband.

'So where can we find him?' Freeman eventually managed to ask when all Anna's apologies had ceased.

'He will be in the pub, The Goosedown, just on the outskirts of Liskeard.'

Without further ado and without explaining any further as to the police progress at the bottom of the pit field, the three detectives left and made their way to the pub.

Freeman and Jeffers knew all about this particular establishment and Soloman was quickly learning.

'Doesn't The Goosedown have a criminal element to its clientele?' Soloman asked, as they drove out of the farmyard.

'Yes, it's where we start, whenever we need to know about stolen property or drugs,' Freeman said succinctly.

Fifteen minutes later they walked into the pub which was full of workmen. This was certainly not a desirable eatery. The landlady could just about manage a simple bar meal, on a good day. The building still smelt of stale ale and cigarette smoke, despite the long term ban on smoking. The carpet was sticky from spilt drinks and the lighting was very dim.

As they entered, the conversation died and the pub went silent. Most of the drinkers, male and female, had dubious connections and all were known to Freeman and Jeffers. Soloman was more of an unknown quantity. Freeman stood inside the door and looked around through the half-light for Harry Winds. He knew who he was looking for, a large man with unkempt sandy coloured hair, a ruddy complexion and a large beer belly. From previous experience he knew that Mr Winds usually took up his daily residence at one end of the bar. However, his usual stool was empty but a half full pint glass stood alone on the bar. Jeffers was about to walk forward to ask the landlady of his whereabouts, when he appeared staggering through a door at the side.

'Oi, Oi, here's trouble,' he cockily said. 'Three of you too, it must be bad.' There was a mocking tone in his voice.

Just what we need at the end of a horrendous day, Soloman thought, a joker.

Freeman started to speak, 'Mr Winds, we have interviewed your wife and sons and now we need to speak with you. Down the station, or back home, your choice?' The question was direct but it had been a long day to say the least and Freeman was in no mood for games or frivolous comments.

'What's it all about?' Mr Winds managed to rally himself.

'Down the station or home?' Freeman reiterated in an even stronger tone.

The pub remained silent, all desperate to know what was happening. They had all known about the closed lane at the bottom of the pit field and the large police presence there. It had been their main topic of conversation that afternoon. They all loved a good gossip.

Realising that he was very much at the centre of attention and not liking it, unless it was on his own terms, he finally said, very quietly.

'Home.'

He was ushered outside and into the police car. He had had far too much to drink to drive himself.

Anna Winds was still looking anxious when the four men arrived back at the farm. She was used to her husband coming home drunk and demanding supper, before collapsing in a heap on the sofa for the remainder of the evening. As a devout Catholic she had pledged to stay with her husband through thick and thin and this was no different to any of the other testing times that her husband had put her through.

The four men settled in the drawing room. Soloman was careful to avoid the rope toy and the half eaten dog chew. Anna, in a bid to placate and ease the tense situation that she sensed, brought in sandwiches and coffee for them all. She retreated to her sanctuary on the other side of the hall. She didn't like her husband getting drunk and in some ways was relieved that the policemen had brought him home. At least for tonight, she wouldn't have to worry. Edward or Howard could collect the Land Rover in the morning.

'Are you aware what has been happening on your land today?' Freeman began.

They all waited for an answer.

'Know you have all been poking your noses into business on my farm.'

'A badly damaged car was found on your land by your sons yesterday. The vehicle identification number reveals that it belongs to missing holiday makers from last summer. What can you tell us about the graves found alongside the pit and the two bodies found there?'

All of a sudden, Harry Winds looked very tired and seemed to have aged ten years. He wasn't used to these prying questions at this time. Why couldn't they just let it all go? They'd found their missing people. It was nothing to do with him, he thought.

He looked up wearily and spoke at last.

'I don't know anything about these bodies, or the car. My sons found it yesterday,' then as an afterthought he added, 'I'm sorry!'

'Sorry for what?' Soloman said, tired of the conversation not leading anywhere.

'That there are bodies on my land,' Harry said. 'What else do you want me to say?'

'The truth would be a good start!' Jeffers interjected.

'I have told you the truth!'

Freeman turned to Jeffers. 'Take a look around, can you?'

149

He gave Jeffers a knowing look, which he understood. He disappeared through the door and voices could be heard between him and Anna on the stairs.

We are going to take your computers and electronic devices for investigation. If you are not involved, as you say, we will get a better picture after they have been analysed by our team.

'Whatever!' Harry said.

It appeared that he had no concerns about two naked corpses that had been found on his land and that had been there for quite some time.

A few minutes later Jeffers appeared in the doorway with three laptops and four mobile phones.

'We won't keep them any longer than needed,' Jeffers said.

There were protestations from Howard and Edward and Anna looked on aghast.

'We'll be in touch,' Freeman said. 'We will let you know our findings and the results from the forensics.'

'You never can tell how people are going to react,' Soloman said as they left the farmyard for the second time that day. 'I suppose being an alcoholic, the topping up kind, he's most probably on another level most of the time.'

The journey back to the police station took twenty minutes.

All three were exhausted but eventually Freeman spoke, 'We will have a catch up meeting in the morning, first thing. Find out forensics initial findings and then Ore,' he used his Christian name on purpose, because what he had to say next was not work related. 'I want you to take the rest of the day and evening off. You look exhausted. We have at last found the Tamworths and their car. Now we have to find out who is responsible but I have a feeling that this is not going to happen overnight.'

'That's very kind boss, are you sure?'

'Yes, I am very sure, then Jeffers can have a night off too, can't have my team exhausting themselves. I will drop you at your door, Ore,' he said as Jeffers climbed out of the car and made his way over to his car on the forecourt.

They all exchanged good nights through the open window. There was now a light rain in the air.

Five minutes later, Ore climbed out of Freeman's car and said good night.

'Make sure you arrange to have a complete break and rest. Do something special. I'll see you in the morning before you go off, at the meeting, nine o'clock sharp.'

Freeman drove off and a very tired Ore fumbled for the outer door key to the vestibule which led to his flat.

'Phone call, shower, quick snack, then bed, he thought as he reached his own door. Once he was inside, he dialled Richard's number.

'Come on, come on,' he said out loud to himself, 'just for once don't be asleep.'

'Hello sweetheart,' a voice purred back, almost instantly, 'I was just thinking about you. You are late, I was going to ring but I know how busy you are at present. Everything alright?'

'Yes, fine thanks, just very tired.' Ore closed his eyes. He felt exhausted.

'Go on,' the gentle voice urged him.

'Can we meet up tomorrow afternoon, I have the afternoon and night off, after an initial meeting first thing. I thought I might come to Bristol to see you. Any chance you might be able to get some time off?'

'I'll see what I can do, leave it with me. Don't leave Bodmin until we have spoken after your meeting, just in case.'

Too tired to ask anything else, Ore simply replied with, 'Okay, that will be fine. I'll look forward to it. Are you alright?'

'Yes, very busy here too. I'll let you go and we will see each other tomorrow.'

Ore managed a quick shower and a piece of toast, before falling into bed. He was asleep when his head touched the pillow.

Chapter 27

The meeting on the following morning was an interesting one. The rest of the team had heard the major news of the discoveries of the previous day and all waited eagerly to hear the findings from forensics. They sat in the meeting room, coffee mugs in hand, waiting for Freeman, Soloman and Jeffers who were going to reveal all.

Soloman had slept well and was looking forward to his day. He just had to get through this meeting.

Freeman recapped in detail how and where the blue Auris car had been found, the interviews with Anna, Edward, Howard and Harry Winds and the gruesome discovery of the two shallow graves and the bodies in the copse by the pit. Then he handed over to Greg and Sue from forensics.

'We believe that the bodies have been in the shallow graves a few months,' Greg began, 'placed there immediately after they disappeared when they failed to return home. The Tamworths were murdered before they were brought to their burial site. There are no signs of a fight, no blows to the head or bruising. Neither are there any broken bones. Our tests lead us to believe that their bodies were brought to the pit and buried there. Whoever did this must have planned this meticulously and known what they were doing. In other words, their deaths were not an accident.'

The note-taking abruptly stopped and a chill ran through the room. It was like stepping into a freezer. Greg looked around the room, half expecting there to be some questions after these revelations. There were none so he carried on.

'However, there are signs of resistance, I should qualify that, by adding that both bodies do show an indication of ligature marks on the ankles and wrists. In summary, there are no signs of resistance in the sense of a fight, but there are signs of some form of restraint. At this stage we don't know if they were held up somewhere, tied up perhaps or,' Greg paused and looked around the room, 'they were restrained voluntarily.'

Greg stopped and sat down. The chill in the room intensified and the team looked around the room at one another, as if looking for clarification.

Jeffers was the first to speak. 'So, what you are saying is that there is a possibility of this being a sexual crime. This would tie in with the fact that we understand that Chris and Bridget did participate from time to time in swinging activity.'

Freeman spoke next. 'Swinging activity, as you put it, doesn't necessarily infer restraint, and that doesn't infer death. We should keep an open mind at this stage and not jump to conclusions. It is a possibility and we can include it in our line of enquiry.' Everyone in the room listened intently. 'Do you have anything to add, Sue?'

'There is one other thing, both bodies have ligature marks around their necks and we can conclude that the cause of death in both bodies is strangulation.'

The chill intensified one more time.

154

'Greg and I would suggest that they were lying down at the time of death, from the angle of the ligature marks, possibly on a bed or something soft. There is no bruising to the backs of the bodies.'

'Any sign of sexual interference or contact?' Jeffers continued. He did not wish his theory to be dismissed or overruled.

'That is possible,' Greg began in answer, 'the bodies have been in the ground a bit too long for us to say at this point but we can investigate that line further.'

Soloman, who was sitting in the front row, then spoke, 'Just to clarify, there are five ligature marks on each body but we are unable to tell if they were held against their will or whether they were compliant in this. It appears that they were lying down and at some point strangled. Then they were moved to the grave site.'

'That is about it, Greg said, 'we are continuing with our tests and will let you know our findings.'

Greg and Sue left the room.

Freeman turned to his team and said, 'Going forward then, our number one priority is to find the culprits. I would suggest that we are looking for a couple. There must have been at least two persons involved to manage the disposal, the burial etc and the removal of the car to the pit. The bodies were buried naked, we have no clothes or personal effects to assist us. The Tamworths' car has been investigated briefly and that too has to be examined more thoroughly. Because the fire burnt the car out completely there is nothing further to help us. No personal effects, nothing! The VIN just confirms that this blue Toyota Auris did belong to the deceased. There is nothing that will lead us to where they went to meet their murderers.'

It was then that Freeman changed tack and spoke directly to Jeffers.

'Ring Chichester. Speak to Willoughby and Oliver-Jones and ask them to send someone around to Simon and Vanessa and fully explain our findings and where we are going next with the investigation. They must be given full support at this horrible time. I think they probably know already but our findings make everything final and complete. It always makes a difference when this final news is made known.'

The other team members were given tasks too. George and Hilary were to look at CCTV again, on the main roads and in the towns to try and trace the movements of the Tamworths' car, from when it first arrived to when it seemingly disappeared. This would be a long and arduous task, because large parts of Cornwall have no CCTV. There would therefore be large gaps in the movement of the car.

Just then, an assistant from the forensics department appeared.

'There's nothing on the Winds' laptops or phones to suggest any connection at all with the deceased. I've taken them back to the front desk to be returned to their owners. Sorry, there are no leads to be found here.'

He backed out of the door, shutting it firmly as if that was his final word on the matter and Freeman let out an involuntary sigh.

'No matter, we have bigger fish to fry at the moment,' he said being surprisingly cheerful.

'Alright if I go now boss?' Soloman said.

'No problem, make sure you have a proper rest.'

Chapter 28

Ore collected his things and made for the stairs. The automatic doors swung open as he approached and he walked out into bright sunshine. After the coolness of the air-conditioned headquarters, even now at the very end of September, it was still warm. It was only a short walk back to his flat and glancing at his watch, he saw that it was approaching eleven o'clock. He would ring Richard and see how he was fixed. He decided that he could be in Bristol soon after lunchtime, if he left immediately.

As he walked along, he tried to gather his thoughts from the earlier meeting.

The forensics team made notes of details and facts, facts that could not be disputed. Certain things, however, did not make sense and needed to be reconciled. He was grateful for the time alone to gather his thoughts.

Words like restraint and resistance had been used almost in the same sentence but they had in fact been used in the sense of opposites. How could there be no resistance unless the murdered couple wanted to be restrained. Forensics said there had been no evidence of a fight, no cuts, bruises or blows to the head, so the only conclusion was that the Tamworths had wanted to be restrained.

The thought made him shudder and gasp. He stood up straight and lengthened his stride, remembering that he was on a public pavement. But the thoughts came back.

If they had wanted to be restrained, then Jeffers' sex theory would be correct. But surely they wouldn't have agreed to a noose around the neck. He could understand the possibility of ankles and wrists being restrained but a ligature around the neck? There were too many ifs and buts here and the whole theory was sort of plausible but how likely? The chance of him being right was, he decided, against all odds and yet it fitted with the facts from forensics.

He reached his front door and unknowingly shook his head. A delivery man held the door for him and Ore was so absorbed that he almost walked into him.

'You alright mate?' the man said.

'Yes thanks, deep in thought.' Ore smiled.

They passed by each other and Ore made his way up the stairs to his flat.

Two minutes later he was on the phone to Richard.

'I've finished work. I could leave now, if you are free later?' Ore began.

'Well, you could, if you really wanted but I shouldn't rush. Unfortunately, I have to be in a meeting until five.'

'What a nuisance,' a strong note of disappointment come through in his voice.

Just then the doorbell rang.

'Hold on a mo, someone at the door,' he continued.

'Bit strange,' he thought. 'I never get unexpected visitors.'

But on opening the door, still holding his phone, there was Richard with a beaming smile, holding his own phone.

'Surprise,' Richard said rather theatrically, 'I thought I would save you a drive. I had time owing so here I am.'

'No meeting then?'

'No, I am here and we have all afternoon and evening, with no interruptions, so we shall put these phones away in your kitchen drawer and they won't be looked at again until I leave.' He continued on at a pace, which made Ore look even more surprised. 'Pack an overnight bag and change out of your work clothes. I'm taking you out to lunch and away for the night. No ifs and no buts, it is all arranged. It's my treat.'

'What a lovely surprise, thank you, are you sure?' was all he managed to say. He suddenly felt very tired after his enlightening meeting and the previous days' events. 'I'll just have a quick shower,' he added grateful that he did not have to drive to Bristol, 'make yourself a coffee.'

Half an hour later and with his overnight bag in hand, Ore left the flat with Richard and they made their way downstairs. The midday warmth was very welcoming as they stepped outside.

'We have been so lucky with the weather this summer,' Ore said looking around for Richard's black hatchback.

Richard meanwhile had walked quickly and was heading towards a large silver blue Mercedes Cabriolet.

'Where's the car?' Ore asked.

'Surprise again,' Richard said even more theatrically than last time. He waved his foot under the rear bumper and at that point the boot lid opened majestically. 'Your case, sir,' he said, gesticulating at the cavernous carpeted area where Ore should place his bag.

'But I don't understand. What has happened to your black car?'

'Oh, that old thing. I thought we would have a treat from now on. This is our new car.' Again, he gesticulated wildly with his right arm at the car.

Ore started to laugh, 'what do you mean, our new car?'

'Our new car means that you are insured to drive this vehicle, which I collected yesterday. I bought her.'

Ore placed his bag in the boot and proceeded to walk around the car.

'She's very pretty. I'm quite struck for words.'

'Well, you don't have to be, just get in and off we will go.'

Richard carefully reversed the car, having lowered the roof, and Ore looked around in wonderment.

Ore had no interest in cars. His parents had always had one but these had tended to be an average family saloon. Ore had grown up believing that cars were for travelling from one place to another. He understood that wealthy people could afford something larger and more expensive but he didn't have an interest, until now. Perhaps it was the smoothness of the engine, the cream leather seats and all those dials. He couldn't believe this day was really happening as they purred along the winding roads. The trees provided a wonderful canopy and when they exited, they alternated with bright sunlight. He felt he was in heaven. He paid no attention to where they were going. Now and then the satnav gave directions.

He placed his head back on the rest and closed his eyes as the large engine powered them along effortlessly and quietly.

They had not long left Bodmin when Richard slowed the car and they turned off the main road into the driveway of The Cove Hotel. Dense rhododendrons lined the drive as it wound this way and that, giving no clue as to what was at the end.

'Where are we going?' Ore asked. He had not seen the sign at the entrance but Richard seemed to know where he was going.

'If you didn't see the sign, then let it be your third surprise.'

A minute later, Richard brought the car to an abrupt standstill. They skidded on the gravel.

'Here we are then,' he announced with a note of finality.

Ore looked around. They were parked outside a large art deco building. A smart sign, Welcome to The Cove Hotel was positioned on the lawn next to the front entrance.

Ore decided at this point that there was something different about Richard. It was obvious that he was very pleased to see him and be in his company again. It would be natural to be excited about their new car and arriving at this hotel. But what else it was, Ore had no idea.

'We have a room booked in the names of Richard Edwards and Ore Soloman,' Richard said a moment later at the front reception desk.

The immaculately smart, tall and efficient young man behind the desk welcomed them graciously and it appeared to Ore that they were being treated with celebrity status.

I imagine this is how things are in this sort of establishment, he thought.

'Welcome to The Cove. My name is Carl and if I can be of any further assistance during your stay, don't hesitate to ask.'

A smile passed across his face as he tapped away at his keyboard as he checked them in. He continued to smile as he led them down a passageway. 'After you, please,' he said to them both as the passageway narrowed. 'You were lucky that we had one room left,' he continued giving Richard a knowing look, his smooth efficiency coming to the fore again.

'Would you like the lift, or do you prefer stairs? The stairs do have the benefit of our wonderful and recently fully restored stained glass window.'

They had stopped now and Richard and Ore looked up at the wide oak stairway and the magnificent window.

'Stairs,' Ore said, before Richard could.

They paused briefly by the window. The bright sun poured through accentuating the vibrant colours. The glass depicted a peaceful wheat field, with the sea in the background.

'Apparently the original builder had the window commissioned. This hotel now stands in that field. Rather a touching idea, don't you think?' Carl said.

Ore and Richard nodded and they all continued.

After a few steps along the wide corridor, Carl stopped outside a door.

'After you,' he again said, having pushed the door open.

They didn't step into a small bedroom as Ore was expecting, it was more of a hallway. On the right were a pair of lift doors and on the left through an archway a large sitting room. There were two sumptuous sofas facing a pair of French doors that opened onto a wide balcony.

'Our Premiere Suite Grande,' Carl said with an energetic flourish, beaming from ear to ear, with his perfect set of white teeth.

'This wonderful room fills many purposes admirably and today I am so pleased that both of you can enjoy it. It was indeed our last vacant room tonight,' he continued on with more flourishes.

'It's just perfect,' Richard said. 'Thank you.'

Ore was speechless and just stood there, locked to the pale grey Wilton.

'Bedroom?' he eventually mumbled.

'Just through here,' Carl said sweeping across the floor, as if he was a member of the English National Ballet. Passing through another archway on the far side of the sitting room, they entered the bedroom, which was just as big as the first area. More bay windows and French doors exited onto the same balcony. In the middle of the room was the bed, a stupendous six foot wide super king. The bedroom and sitting room areas were decorated in a modern style and as such the bed was a low affair. Ore looked around and took it all in.

'Completely refurbished last year,' Carl said, reading Ore's mind. 'Took six months to complete, by a team from London. They do the Rocco Forte Group.' He spoke enthusiastically and was obviously very proud of this room and enjoyed showing it off.

'Thank you very much,' Ore finally said. 'It's all perfect.'

With that Carl left and the door was quietly closed.

'Well,' Richard said. 'I am pleased you like it.'

'You knew, didn't you?' Ore said.

'I had an inkling,' Richard replied with a wide smile, 'I knew it wasn't the little room around the back, above the bins next to the kitchen cooking vents.

'Thank you again,' Ore said.

'It is even better than I thought, better than our best suite in Bristol,' Richard said, looking around again.

'Shall we have something to eat? Ore said, 'you know me, I need feeding every few hours.'

'There is a very nice beach bar serving food all day next to the terrace. Fancy it?'

'Lead on.'

Together they made their way down this time in the lift, whereupon they found themselves in a large ground floor sitting room, complete with coffee machine and more French doors leading on to a private terrace and garden.

'I believe this room is used for wedding guests to assemble before making their way onto the terrace or garden or even the beach for ceremonies. If the weather is inclement, ceremonies can be performed in here. The bride can come down from her suite upstairs in complete privacy and make her entrance here. It is all part of the Premiere Suite Grande.'

Ore was wide-eyed again.

'Come on,' Richard said teasingly, 'you need food before you have one of your funny turns.'

They made their way through the French doors onto the terrace, through a side gate and then into the beach bar.

The rest of the afternoon continued in a haze of sitting in the sunshine, eating, drinking and a walk along the beach that lay under some low cliffs, accessed from the hotel's grounds via stone steps. It couldn't have been more perfect, the sun shone and the sky and sea were a deep blue. As they neared the end of the beach, Ore decided that it was warm enough for a quick swim. No one else had walked this far so he stripped off and raced into the water. Ore was a strong swimmer and pounded through the waves. After ten minutes he swam back to the beach.

'Awake now,' he said as he raced back to Richard, who had been watching, sitting out of the wind behind a large rock.

'A bit taken by the moment,' he said when he had his breath back. 'No towel! I'll just have to dry here in the sun, next to you, like a wet dog.'

They had dinner in the hotel restaurant that evening. The hotel was full and after dinner they joined the other guests in the bar. It was a warm evening and there was a Mediterranean feel to the night. A relaxed calm had fallen on The Cove and all its guests.

Chapter 29

Ore and Richard slept well, amidst the rumpled linen bed clothes. The cool sea air flowed through the windows and the sound of the distant waves lapping on the beach, soothed and calmed.

Ore slept so peacefully that he never heard Richard leave the room. He was eventually woken by a squawking seagull. He lay there, unperturbed, thinking how lucky he was. His thoughts floated away from the unsolved case that he had worked on so tirelessly. Although it no longer had premier status, it never seemed too distant from his thoughts and he often wondered how Simon and Vanessa were coping.

He sat up in bed and to his dismay, saw that there was no sun, only sea mist. He couldn't see the beach or sea and even the grounds below seemed to be quickly disappearing into the mizzle.

Where was Richard? He thought, bathroom, I expect.

He called out but there was no reply.

Just then he heard a deep voice.

'Room service.'

Before he had time to answer, the door opened at the far end and Ore heard the 'chink, chink' of a breakfast trolley being wheeled across the Wilton, towards the bedroom.

'Mr Edwards requested room service breakfast for you both. Shall I leave the trolley here?' Carl said, parking the breakfast next to the bed. 'Mr Edwards will only be a few moments, he said to tell you that he had to make some work calls, something cropped up.'

'Thank you so much,' Ore said. 'I really appreciate breakfast being brought to the room. I had better get up, got to be back at work shortly.'

'It's my pleasure,' Carl said. 'Relax and enjoy, sorry about the mizzle.' Another flash of dazzling white teeth and the tall apparition was gone as quickly and efficiently as he had arrived.

Ore had never had a room service trolley brought to him before and was just helping himself to some of the cooked delights, under the huge silver dome, when Richard reappeared through the door.

'Been with the manager, sorting out a problem at Bristol.'

'Is this hotel part of your group?' Ore asked

'Might be!' Richard replied, with a big smile.

'So that's how you managed to book this room. It all fits now.'

'Not exactly. It is part of our group I admit, but this room really was the last one. No one was getting married yesterday or today and no famous guests wanted it either. It was therefore available to anyone.'

167

Ore felt totally relaxed and was enjoying his breakfast, but all too soon it was time to leave and after reluctantly leaving the suite, they made their way downstairs. Having thanked Carl, who was again on reception, they left the hotel.

'Mizzle is just clearing a bit now. Perhaps the tide is on the turn.' Ore said, peering into the diminishing wetness.

'You're driving,' Richard answered. 'You'll need this.'

He handed Ore the key fob. 'Just put it in your pocket. It will start at the touch of the button.'

Having gone over the rudimentaries of such a complex car, Ore dropped the roof and reversed out of their space and they made their way back up the drive. It was quite different to anything he had driven before and once on the open road he realised the immense power under the expanse of bonnet. He was equally grateful for the effortless braking, as he looked down and realised that he was exceeding the local speed limit.

Mustn't let this go to my head, he thought. Wouldn't be good to be caught on camera.

The journey back seemed to take only half the time it had taken to arrive at The Cove yesterday. By the time they were parking at Ore's flat, he felt in a complete daze. So much had happened in the last twenty-four hours and there had been so many new experiences.

'Better get changed quickly,' he said, 'then you can drop me at the station. I'll try not to look too loved up as I climb out of a silver blue convertible. Thank you so much Richard. It's been fantastic.'

Twenty minutes later Ore Soloman was climbing out of the Mercedes, outside the police headquarters. He was down to earth with a bump.

'See you again, very soon I hope.'

They embraced and Richard drove off back to Bristol.

Chapter 30

After that all-important and revealing meeting the day before, Jeffers made his way back to his desk and pondered how best to deal with the task that Freeman had given him. He was to inform Simon and Vanessa of the findings of their parents' bodies and their burnt out car.

Simon and Vanessa must realise that there would be a strong likelihood that their parents were now dead but the circumstances and situation would not be an easy message to give. Thankfully it would not be him delivering the news.

He dialled the direct number for DI Willoughby and was pleased that she answered almost immediately.

He gave her the news and she efficiently made notes.

'Yes of course, we will arrange to speak with them later today.'

'There are no more details about the exact nature of their deaths. I think that the information that you have will be enough for any teenagers to hear, let alone accept. We will have to hope that the culprits reveal all when we catch them. We are getting there slowly.

At least now, when forensics have finished, the bodies can be released for burial or cremation. That is of course, as long as they are conclusive in their findings, otherwise we may have to wait until after a court case. I wish you well and keep in touch.'

With that they ended their call and Jeffers was deeply relieved.

It's all part of my job, Michelle Willoughby thought, the absolute worst part. I will see if DS Oliver-Jones is up to doing the telling. It's all part of her training.

Willoughby went in search of Oliver-Jones and finding her at her desk, she sat down and went through it all with her.

'That's just so terrible,' was her response at the end. 'Do you want me to tell them?'

DI Willoughby was grateful that she had offered.

'I will of course come with you and step in at any moment. I'll phone the school and let them know that we are on our way and to prepare a room for us. You phone the leisure centre and arrange for us to collect Simon. We will take him to the school and tell them both there.'

The relevant calls were made and they set off for the leisure centre.

Simon was waiting for them, by the main entrance. He looked tired, pensive, pale and considerably older than his nineteen years.

'It's bad news, isn't it?' he said as he climbed into the back.

'We'll tell you about everything when you are both together.'

'I know but the wait has been unbearable. Vanessa's hardly speaking to me. I've tried asking her friend's mum and she says that even she can get nothing out of her.'

171

As they drew up at the school, Simon began to shake.

'Need some air,' he said, as he stumbled forward out of the car.

He leaned forward resting his hands on his thighs and took in deep breaths of air.

'In your own time,' Willoughby said, 'no rush.'

A few moments later he straightened up, 'I'm okay now.'

They made their way into the building and were met by the head receptionist. She had been advised of their impending arrival and showed them into a side room. They did not have to wait long for Vanessa. She was ushered in by the school counsellor, looking drained and tired.

DS Oliver-Jones began, 'I'm sorry that we don't have good news for you. Yesterday, two bodies were found in a shallow grave together, in Cornwall, not too far away from where your parents were staying. The forensic team have been working tirelessly since the discovery and we are now certain that they are the bodies of your father and mother.'

At this point, Vanessa let out a small scream and burst into sobbing tears. Simon followed suit and the room was hushed, save for the sobbing. The counsellor put her arms around Vanessa and cuddled her. She hardly moved, except for the shaking created by her sobbing. DI Willoughby put her arm around Simon and after five minutes he rallied.

'How long had they been in this grave?'

'Forensics believe that they were buried about the time they went missing, about 3 months,' Willoughby said very gently.

'But how were they killed and why?' Vanessa asked.

DS Oliver-Jones looked at the counsellor who gave a nod to intimate that it was good to give all the answers now.

'It's not a good situation I'm afraid,' Oliver-Jones began, 'and it might be best to wait until you have come to terms a little more with this current news. The main thing is that your parents have been found. We know at last what has happened to them.'

She looked at both the teenagers for confirmation that she should proceed. Simon stood up and put his arms around his sister. Their strong bond was evident.

'We should wait Vee and take this bit in first. Best to follow the advice of the police. They know best.'

'I need to know now, Si,' she implored.

'Very well, whatever you want.'

DS Oliver-Jones then explained very gently about the possible strangulation. She spoke about the connection with the swingers and briefly touched on the possible restraint issues. It was much better, on reflection to speak of these matters now, in a safe environment and with support around them. Simon and Vanessa could be badly affected through the strong powers of social media. Measures could now be put in place to help protect them. Vanessa seemed to be satisfied with the answers. Perhaps it was all so much that she didn't really hear. She was at least quiet now.

It was nearly lunchtime and it was immediately decided that Vanessa need not return to class. She would be off school for a few weeks and the counsellor would provide full support and keep a regular eye on how she was coping.

Simon rang the leisure centre and he was excused all duties until further notice.

The school counsellor took Vanessa and Simon home. As they had no family, social services were advised and they also agreed to keep an eye on them both.

'You did well in an exceptionally difficult circumstance,' Willoughby said to Oliver-Jones a little later as they drove back to the police station.

'It was the hardest thing I have ever had to do,' Oliver-Jones said, near to tears herself now that the enormity of what she had just done overcame her. She sobbed quietly in the passenger seat, while Willoughby drove.

'That's alright. Best to let it all out. Gone are the days when the police had no feelings. It was especially hard bearing in mind their ages and the fact that they have no other family. Going forward for them will be a real challenge. It is the most horrible situation.' Willoughby concluded.

Chapter 31

Mrs Doris Silvers had lived in Liskeard all her life. She was now a stout and upright seventy seven years old. Her best friend was Sylvia Jago. They were the same age though she was slightly less stout and upright. They had grown up together, having been first introduced at junior school. Since that moment a certain bond had developed and grown. Their lives had twisted and turned like everyone else's, but through thick and thin, they had remained the closest of friends.

They knew all the gossip and everyone who lived locally. They had lived in the same houses, one street apart, for all of their married lives and shared everything. Never did a day go by that they weren't in and out of each other's neat and tidy homes. It was almost as if they were sisters. Sylvia Jago had sadly lost her husband ten years before and Doris Silvers had lost her dear Eric just a year ago. They were now even more supportive of each other.

Doris Silvers still drove, whilst Sylvia Jago did not. Doris was therefore supremely useful to Sylvia for all those trips that were too difficult or made awkward by the dwindling numbers of buses. When Doris was not available, Sylvia called upon the services of her son to ferry her about.

It was now mid-October and the day had started with sunshine.

That's good, thought Doris, I can walk into town, rather than take Eric. Since Eric her husband had passed away, she had fondly started to call her trusty but now very ancient Ford Fiesta car by the same name. Whilst driving, she would hold a one-sided conversation out loud.

'Come along Eric, get us up this hill' and 'come along Eric, help me park.'

Although a little odd, Doris found this a comfort and did not care what other drivers thought, as they saw an elderly lady apparently talking to herself. Even Sylvia had got used to it, for Doris did not reserve these conversations for her solo journeys.

Many of the leaves had turned a golden brown and Doris had spent the last few days raking and sweeping those that had fallen in her garden. She had had breakfast and was preparing to leave. Her walk into town would take about fifteen minutes. She collected her straight raincoat from the hall cupboard and her plain brown court shoes. This she considered her smart wear, suitable for visiting her best friend's son, at the motor repair garage that he owned. She always liked to dress smart, as she put it, when in town. One never knew who one was likely to meet.

She set off at her usual brisk and upright pace, handbag in the crook of her elbow. She had telephoned Sylvia the night before, to check that Thomas Jago would be in his garage office, at ten thirty precisely. He would be and promised his mother that he would have the kettle on for Doris' arrival. The content of her meeting remained a mystery to him. His son, Andy, had only recently serviced the car and fitted four new tyres.

Perhaps, he thought, she is coming to discuss finding a replacement car. He had after all been suggesting the need to change Eric, for a few years.

At ten thirty precisely, Thomas Jago heard the all too familiar sound of those court shoes approaching the office. He flipped the switch on the kettle and waited.

'Good morning Thomas. I am here about a certain invoice. I need it for my records and sadly my dog Teddy shredded it, whilst I was on the telephone. I am sorry to bother you but you know how these things trouble me.'

Doris sat down on the one available chair. She had known Thomas all her life and felt she did not need to ask permission.

'It's the receipt for the last service and four new tyres,' she said precisely. 'You can find it on your computer thingy,' she said, waving her handbag at Thomas' screen.

'Just in case you can't,' she continued on, not trusting the power of a computer, 'it was at the end of June, I think. I don't remember things that well nowadays. You were not here and it was very busy. Far more so than Andy should really have to manage on his own.' She gave Thomas a disapproving look as if to say that he had no business ever leaving the garage. She peered over her glasses at him. 'The garage was filled with holiday-makers. They always come in multiples.' She rattled on but Thomas was used to Doris. In many respects she had been like a formidable aunt to him, for all his life and didn't he know about her addiction to correct paperwork. This wasn't a one-off request. He should have guessed that their meeting would have been paperwork-based. 'They do wear strange clothes, some of the holiday-makers. I'm not a prude but some of the outfits would be more suited to one of those nightclub places, not that I've ever been to one.'

'What sort of clothes?' Thomas found himself asking out of politeness.

'Short skirts and lots of red,' Doris said without a moment's pause.

'What did you say?' Thomas said, rather too abruptly.

177

'I said, I need the paperwork for the last service, which Teddy shredded yesterday afternoon.'

Teddy was her golden Labrador and full-time trusty companion, for all the times that Sylvia was not present.

'Yes,' Thomas said very quickly, 'after that, the bit about short skirts and lots of red.' A worrying bell was ringing in the back of his mind. 'I think perhaps I will look at the CCTV to check who came into the garage on that day. I can work out the day and date,' he said cautiously. His mind was filling with worry and doubt. 'Do you perhaps remember the disappearance of two holiday-makers from Liskeard in June and all the television coverage of it? They kept mentioning a red jacket. Doris, don't you remember seeing it all on the television?'

Doris' jaw dropped at the thought that she might have missed some scandal which had happened right in her midst.

'I don't remember much these days,' she repeated, 'unless it directly involves me. You mean I might have been involved in a crime?'

Despite the mounting excitement in her voice, she was becoming concerned that she might be in trouble, or that she could have been more helpful to the police. That would be the last straw.

'I'll sort your paperwork out and drop it round, Doris, but now I really must check the CCTV.'

At the sound of such excitement, Doris replied, 'Can't I stay?'

'I really think it would be best if you went home. I promise I will let you and Mum know all about it, now please...'

He could sense Doris' reluctance to leave but having received a knowing stare from Thomas she stood abruptly and gathering up her bag, she made to leave.

'It'll be okay, Doris. I'll sort it, nothing more for you to do here.'

She left the building, muttering something about, 'not being allowed to finish her tea.'

Thomas closed the office door and started to look at the CCTV. It did not take him long before he had found the right day and scrolling slowly through he soon saw the unmistakeable figure of Doris Silvers. At first she was on camera looking over in the direction of where her car was parked. The footage showed a group standing close to her, and as he focused in on the group he could quite clearly see a woman wearing an unusual jacket. As he studied the screen further, the woman and the man next to her turned around and the front of the jacket could not be mistaken for anything other than the jacket that had appeared on the TV screen so many times a few months before.

Thomas wasted no time in calling the hotline number for this crime. He had a good relationship with the local community officer who always left an A5 poster relating to any particular crime, relevant to the area.

It was Jessica who answered at the Bodmin headquarters. She took all the details and promised to send someone immediately.

'I will try to find the bill with an address for whoever is showing on the footage.' Thomas said. 'I am sorry this has only just come to light. I wasn't here that afternoon, being at the dentist, and my son Andy, who was here, is not a people person and doesn't notice people, only car engines. I'll have a word with him in the meantime, see if I can jog his memory. I've been following this case on the news but had no idea that I might be able to help until now. I'm sorry!'

Chapter 32

Jessica had logged that call at ten past eleven and by eleven thirty, Freeman and Soloman were on their way to Jago Motors.

They had been dealing with routine matters that morning and had to quickly change tack and re-focus on the old case.

The weather had deteriorated and the early sun had changed into rain. The roads were now saturated and the leaves had turned after the heat of that fabulous summer. Most had fallen and lay strewn at the roadsides.

Freeman broke the silence as they drove at speed toward Liskeard. 'I really feel this may be the breakthrough that we have been waiting for. If we have CCTV footage of a woman in a red jacket, we will also have a time that they were still alive and hopefully we can track their movements after that.'

They reached Jago Motors and found Thomas Jago studiously concentrating on his CCTV monitor. He barely looked up when the two police officers introduced themselves and showed their warrant cards. Freeman sat down on the one chair.

Soloman began, 'Before we look at the CCTV, can you tell us again exactly what this lady said to you and why you haven't come forward sooner.'

Thomas Jago looked up and repeated again, exactly what Doris Silvers had said to him. He hadn't come forward because he had had no need to look at his CCTV footage and in any case, he had been at the dentist, on that particularly busy afternoon. It was only his conversation with Doris that morning that had prompted his call to the police. His son Andy, rarely watched the news and in any case he wouldn't have noticed any of their customers, let alone a woman in a red leather jacket.

'We will have to speak with both your son and this Mrs Silvers,' Soloman continued.

'I'll call Andy into the office now.'

He was a tall spotty lad, wearing a beanie hat. The sleeves of his oily overalls were rolled up, revealing full tattoos on both arms.

'What can you tell us about the afternoon in question, when your father was at the dentist and you had full responsibility for the business?'

'I know Mrs Silvers very well but I know her car better. I think it was quite busy that afternoon. She kept asking questions about her Fiesta, which I had serviced and fitted with four new tyres. There wasn't any need because she knows that she can trust us completely. There were several groups of people, I seem to remember, not just one person per car. They were all milling around and getting in my way, between checking them in, sorting their vehicles out and then taking their money. I never looked at any of them or noticed anything different. You'll see all that on the CCTV.'

'My son is a good chap, trustworthy and a hard worker. I wouldn't have left him, if I had any such concerns. The takings are always correct and there's never been any bother.' Thomas Jago said, chipping in his thoughts.

'That'll do for now,' Freeman said looking at Andy, 'We'll look at the CCTV and come back to you if we need to.'

The three men peered at the screen. Andy had been quite correct, there did seem to be a multitude of groups coming and going that afternoon. At this point Thomas Jago explained that most of these groups would have been families or friends, on holiday. 'Something has gone wrong with the car or a tyre, and they all pile out and wait for it to be fixed,' he said in summary.

A few cups of coffee later and after Andy had been sent out for sandwiches, the CCTV was now showing two thirty in the afternoon. There had been a lull over the lunch time period but after that the chaos had started again. It appeared that Doris Silvers had arrived to pick up her car when a small red Fiat had pulled onto the forecourt. The front nearside tyre was looking almost flat and in less than half an hour, it would have been un-driveable. The driver was seen getting out followed by three others. In total there were two men and two women.

'Well by the look of them, they are on holiday but it seems a little odd that four adults should all get out of such a small car,' Thomas Jago said. 'Of course, we are just here to mend cars and get people back on their travels, not analyse their clothing and whether the vehicle is the norm for carrying four adults.'

'Yes,' Soloman said, 'that is more part of our job, when the necessary situation arises.'

They all peered at the screen again and although it was only in black and white, one of the women was in a very distinctively styled jacket. Freeman searched for the photo that Simon Tamworth had sent of his parents on that amazing Italian holiday a few years ago, when his Dad had bought the red jacket for his dear wife. There was certainly a very good likeness between the couple in the photograph and one of the men and one of the women on the CCTV footage.

'I think we might have our couple,' Freeman said, sitting back and sounding very pleased. 'What address did the driver give and what's that registration? While we get those details, ring Jeffers and ask him to visit Mrs Silvers as soon as possible to see if she can add anything further. He'll be much better than me at that. I'm all fired up now and ready to sort this out finally, once and for all.'

Soloman went outside and sat in the car to make the call to Jeffers. He gave the address and described what Mrs Silvers had purported to have seen, on the day in question.

Ten minutes later, having gained the car registration and the address, Freeman and Soloman left Jago Motors and drove to Looe. They now had two new pieces of information. A car registration number gave them the details of the car, a small red Fiat, registered to a Mr Brocking and an address in Looe which appeared to be a holiday let. The name of the property was Treworthy Cottage. When the car registration was run through the police national computer, a third piece of vital information would be revealed, a home address. This would be the breakthrough that they had long been waiting for.

'Ring Jessica,' Freeman barked and get her to run the registration through the computer.' Soloman did as he was asked.

It was happening just as Jeffers had said to Soloman on their trip to Brighton. 'It only takes one small unsuspecting conversation, a word said that the speaker has no preconceived idea will be of any help and the jigsaw pieces all fall neatly into place.'

Jessica was back in an instant and stated that the car was registered to an address near Tintagel. Freeman decided that rather than rushing straight in to where Mr Brocking lived, it might be better to visit Treworthy Cottage first. Being in Looe, it appeared to Freeman and Soloman that this was the more likely place for the crime to have been committed. It was closer to the burial site and the pit where the car had been abandoned. Mr Brocking's apparent home address where the car was registered, was thirty miles away on the north coast.

Further clues might also be revealed by a visit to this holiday cottage. Freeman and Soloman would be more conclusively armed, when they finally called on Mr Brocking.

Chapter 33

Freeman and Soloman found the road where Treworthy Cottage was located from the post code. To his dismay, Soloman recognised it immediately as Harbour Street, the very street that he and Richard had walked down in June. He went quiet but for the moment Freeman did not notice. They drove very slowly, past the theatre, looking to the left and the right for the house name. They passed the art gallery on the right with its little car park and continued on down, towards the harbour. They were about to turn around and re-trace their way back up the street, when they saw there on the left, a small terraced property with a tiny frontage, just two paces deep. There next to the door, was a name plate. Freeman read it out aloud, 'Treworthy Cottage managed by Sea Breeze Holiday Homes.' Soloman pulled himself together and having parked the car, he and Freeman ran back up the street.

'Get onto this, Sea Breeze Holiday Homes, now,' he barked at Soloman who was getting used to the manner in which he was given orders.

Soloman made the call and told the manager that it was imperative that he dropped everything and came immediately to the property.

Ten minutes later, a short stocky man with fair thinning hair, in his forties appeared on foot. He was breathless and took a moment before he could speak.

'I am the manager of Sea Breeze Holiday Cottages. David Watson, how do you do?' he held his hand out but it was ignored. 'I came as quickly as I could, what's the urgency? Someone not well inside? Has an ambulance been called?'

'Nothing quite like that,' Freeman said, taking charge. 'Come and sit in the car for a minute, would you, and we will explain.'

Freeman spoke in detail. Mr Watson absorbed the information slowly and looked visibly shocked. One of the cottages on his books was now being fully implicated in what had been on the minds of the local community for the past four months. Eventually he managed to unlock the door and let the policemen inside. The cottage was let this week and just as had happened before, the current holiday makers were called and asked to return. The cleaners, Tara and Ben Longworth, were also telephoned. Then Mr Watson called the owners, Nigel and Sue Rathbone, who lived diagonally across the road. They also ran the art gallery.

It all seemed a bit close to home for Soloman who was remembering how he and Richard had walked down this street and spent time peering at the paintings in the window.

Nigel Rathbone appeared first.

'What on earth is going on here? he shouted as he came through the door. 'What is all this about?'

Before anyone had time to speak to him, Greg and Sue arrived and walked past him and straight into the kitchen.

'What's happening here, Freeman?' Greg calmly asked.

Soloman took him aside and explained the situation. They were to give the property a complete and thorough check.

Freeman spoke to Nigel Rathbone and by the time he had finished, Mr Rathbone was certainly quieter and hung his head with worry over the possible implications that his lovely and charming property was the scene of a horrible and deadly crime.

'My wife and I were out of the country at the time of these incidents. We came in here the morning after we got back and didn't see anything out of place. Tara and Ben always do an excellent job of our changeovers between guests and they didn't report anything to us either.

'We will adjourn to the Rathbone's home across the street so that forensics can start to work on this property,' Freeman said, calling everyone to attention.

They were just on the point of leaving when the current guests appeared at the front door. They were amazed at the number of people who had assembled at the cottage. The situation was explained and somehow they seemed very understanding. They were not given the full details, but after all the television coverage in the summer, it would not take much to work out the connection. It was with relief that they heard they could spend the rest of their week's holiday in the neighbouring hotel, The Castle, at the bottom of Harbour Street.

David Watson escorted them there directly and settled them in. He was grateful that they did not complain at the prospect of having their plans changed. He then made his way back to Tinterdale House, the home of the Rathbones. A full discussion was proceeding with Nigel and Susan, his wife, and Tara and Ben Longworth. None were under any suspicion. The Rathbones could prove that they were out of the country until after the guests had left. Mr Watson could not be implicated either because he had been away that weekend in Manchester at his wife's parents' golden wedding anniversary celebrations. The Longworth's explained that they had not seen any guests when they had arrived at nine thirty to clean.

It became clear from the booking that in addition to Trevor Brocking, the other guest at Treworthy Cottage was a Ms Sonia Upton. Their home address was at a remote location near Tintagel.

After interviewing all those connected, Freeman and Soloman made their way back to the cottage to see what progress Greg and Sue had made. As with the other cottage in Liskeard, they had started in the loft and were working their way down. Police incident tape surrounded the front of the house and a policeman stood guard outside.

Locals and holiday makers had started to gather wondering what was happening and soon a TV camera crew and some reporters appeared on the scene.

Freeman gave a short statement to the gathering crowd in a vain effort to move them on, 'we are making enquiries at this property, concerning a possible past crime. There is nothing for any of you here. A further statement will be released later. I would ask that you move away and let us continue our investigations, unimpeded.'

Turning to Soloman after he had finished, he continued, 'ask Mike Jeffers and Patrick Hill to start conducting house to house enquiries and find out the results of Jeffers' meeting with Doris Silvers.'

Freeman and Soloman returned to their parked car and waited for Jeffers and Hill. It was now mid-afternoon and Soloman got the distinct impression that it was going to be yet another long day. He had wanted to have a long chat with Richard that evening but decided to take five minutes now and wonder down to the front. It would be like a mini trip down a rather recent memory lane, he thought.

Five minutes later he was sitting on the seafront with a coffee in his hand.

'Guess where I am?' he said when Richard answered. 'I'm on the beach front in Looe, where we were in the summer and the sun is shining again after earlier rain. Can't say much but that big case has been re-opened. It's very ironic that it was all happening supposedly when we were here. I can't believe it.'

The conversation continued with how Richard was coping with a large delegation of Japanese businessmen and their wives, who were staying in the hotel.

'I'm having to do a crash course in understanding Japanese etiquette and culture and pass it on to all the staff here. We are having daily mini training sessions, so that we don't make any faux pas.'

'Good luck with it all,' Ore said, promising to arrange a meet up sooner rather than later, when he was less busy. The call was finished and he drained his coffee cup.

Soloman returned to the car to find that Freeman was explaining everything that had happened and was advising how Jeffers and Hill should conduct the house to house enquiries.

'I'm not expecting much but there might be something. Anything at all will be a help. It is after all several months ago,' Freeman finally said, as Jeffers and Hill climbed out of the car and made for the neighbouring cottages.

Chapter 34

Earlier on in the day, Jeffers had gone to visit Doris Silvers. He didn't mind being sent on these more sensitive errands.

To achieve the best results, he needed to tread very carefully. He had heard all about Doris Silvers but as it turned out, he need not have had any concerns. Pleased to have some company, she was quite a sweetheart, rather at odds with how she had been described.

He drew up outside and was surprised that the address led him to a three bedroom bungalow, built in the early 1960's. He had been expecting an older house. Doris and Eric had moved there when they were first married. The house was brand new then. She hadn't moved and was very proud of her home and garden. After Eric had died, she had even had a new bathroom fitted. There wasn't anything wrong with the original: it was just a little dated in colour and styling. The primrose yellow was now gone and in its place was a gleaming white suite.

Jeffers walked up the path and was leaning forward to ring the doorbell, when the front door was opened with a flourish.

'I know who you are,' Doris said. 'I've been expecting the police since this morning.'

Jeffers was slightly taken aback, usually people were looking for an excuse not to let the police in, not welcome them with open arms and frogmarch them over the threshold. He was directed into the sitting room at the rear of the bungalow, overlooking the garden and to an exact chair, whilst Doris went to the kitchen to make one tea for herself and one coffee, 'with two sugars please,' Jeffers had added.

When out and about, Doris Silvers worked hard to be noticed. She felt that the community needed the benefit of her ample wisdom and advice. When at home, everything was different. Doris became less overbearing, more human and there was a warmth in her manner.

She brought the tea and coffee into the sitting room and before Jeffers could start his questioning, Doris began, 'Aren't my begonias wonderful, such a good year, but my dahlias and hydrangeas haven't been so good since Eric passed away.'

She paused for breath and Jeffers took his opportunity to speak, 'Your garden is beautiful but I am here about the time you collected your car from Jago Motors. I am referring to when you had it serviced at the end of June. Do you remember a small red Fiat?'

'Well I don't know cars, except my own. Thomas, down the garage, this morning did seem to become rather enthused when I mentioned that the holiday makers seem to wear rather inappropriate clothing. When I went to collect the car, now I think back I do remember someone in a distinctive red jacket. I didn't think any more about it, as I just wanted to get away from all the crowds and those holidaymakers. She got out of a small red car with another woman and two chaps. Flat tyre I think.' The last comment was an indication as to what Doris thought was wrong with the car. 'That's it really, I was pleased to get out. It was such a hot day and very stuffy in that waiting room. I had to get Eric home and start on the watering. I never saw the car or the occupants again.' She leaned forward on

191

the edge of her armchair and spoke in a soft whisper. There wasn't anyone around who could possibly have heard but Doris liked to add a touch of drama. 'They say this might have something to do with the disappearance of those two holidaymakers in the summer.'

'That's as maybe but did you hear them speak, anything that they might have said?' Freeman sat poised with his iPad ready to take notes.

Doris was still sitting on the edge of her seat holding her teacup in mid-air. She thought for a moment, 'No, I didn't hear them say anything, no wait, I think I heard one of the chaps say that he hoped that they would not have to wait too long. It was so hot in there, I had to leave.'

'Nothing else then?' he said coaxingly.

Mrs Silvers decided not to answer. She was far more interested to find out if there was any gossip. 'Nothing you can tell me then?' She leaned further forward again, anticipating some news-worthy item. She smiled knowingly.

Jeffers smiled back and rising swiftly to his feet, he said 'I am sorry that I can't say anymore but thank you for your help and for the coffee.' He backed down the hallway, declining a second cup, and was relieved to step outside.

He drove back to Looe and Harbour Street.

Chapter 35

The house-to-house enquiries did not reveal anything more. Harbour Street in June was always busy with tourists and the locals usually kept their heads down and got on with their own day to day living. They knew that the town had to have tourists in order to survive but they worked around the visitors, getting used to and accepting different cultures and noise levels.

Harbour Street was always busy with traffic and even questions regarding any unusual traffic, late at night or early in the morning, were greeted with remoteness and indifference. Guests from up country quite often arrived in the early hours, having been given the codes to key safes. Revving of engines, doors slamming umpteen times were all quite usual as were raised and excited voices, happy to be by the seaside after a long journey. It was the same when they left, sorry to be leaving but eager to beat the traffic on the way home.

When they called at the cottage belonging to Mr Brooker, who baked for The Castle Hotel, he couldn't remember anything out if the ordinary either, even though he was up late at night and again early in the morning. In the busy season, noise was his enemy and he had learnt to block it out, when he could.

Some of the shopkeepers vaguely recognised the woman in the red leather jacket from the photographs and the footage from the CCTV but it seemed that no one could remember on which day.

It was now well past ten pm and Freeman and Soloman had gained very little extra information. They were however armed with as much information as possible, before they visited their suspects. Tomorrow was another day.

Chapter 36

Although late, DCI Freeman called his Superintendent Louise Marshall. He felt that they should visit Mr Brocking very early the following morning. Freeman needed authorisation for back up, possibly armed and wanted everything ready in advance for his surprise visit.

During the night hours, much preparation was put in place. Maps were sourced and roads checked, the terrain around the suspects' house was scrutinised and records were checked to see if Mr Brocking and his live-in partner Sonia Upton had been in trouble before. Guns and ammunition were released from security and specialist uniforms were sought from the back of lockers and cupboards. Tactics were discussed and a route to the property organised.

After a few hours' sleep and a final briefing, they all set off.

Freeman and Soloman led the group in the first car, Jeffers and Hill behind. The armed response team followed in several other vehicles.

Superintendent Louise Marshall was up and about early too, at her desk with a direct radio link.

It was still dark when they set off at five thirty am. The route to Tintagel was due to take forty minutes. It was a damp morning and the roads were wet after several rain showers in the night. This added to the impending gloom of the task ahead. The wind turbines on the top road were not rotating. It was as if the negativity of the situation was affecting everything. The team already knew about the unusual terrain around the target property.

They turned into the final road. It was a narrow lane. Light was just filtering through the darkness but it was shrouded in trees on both sides and the darkness descended again. The lane dropped gently down and the convoy of vehicles slowed. Where was this property? On one side was a rocky cliff face covered in ferns and ivy, on the other the lane gripped the edge of a small but very deep valley. It was filled with trees and far down at the bottom a small stream meandered this way and that, sometimes splashing and sometimes crashing amongst the mossy rocks.

The convoy stopped and Freeman and Soloman got out of their car. Engines were turned off and there was as eerie silence as they walked further down the lane and looked up and down over the wall by the roadside.

Just ahead was a small layby. Was it a passing place on this narrow lane, or a parking place, perhaps indicating a property somewhere? There was no sign of any vehicles but as they looked more closely, they could just make out a small cottage nestling on the valley floor, amongst the trees and rocks. It was a foreboding place and now a mizzle was stealthily and silently creeping towards them.

Soloman noticed a little wisp of smoke rising vertically from a lone chimney pot. Someone was inside. On the other side of the lane, a few yards further down and tucked amidst the rock face was an old wooden shed. The roof was collapsing and there was only one of a pair of doors. Large ferns grew all around it. The walls and door were green with age, damp and neglect. Soloman walked quickly over, whilst Freeman was studying the cottage below, formulating a plan.

Quickening his pace, he soon reached the shed. A pair of well-worn car tracks indicated that this was used as a garage, the one door being in the closed position. It would have to be a very small car, as the width of the space and the small depth in between the rocks indicated.

Soloman felt his heartbeat quicken. As he drew closer he saw what he was hoping for. He could just make out the back half of a small red car. He peered inside; the registration number was the same as he had previously memorised. It looked as if Mr Brocking was at home this morning.

Soloman raced back to Freeman, bounding very quietly on his toes.

'The car we are looking for is here in a small shed further down the lane,' he said, pointing hurriedly in the direction he had just come from.

'I thought it probably would be,' Freeman said, breaking his own silence. 'Better get down there.' He pointed towards the cottage. 'You and I to the front door, Jeffers and Hill round the back. Get the team down there too, as we discussed.'

Soloman moved back quickly to the vehicles and marshalled everyone to their allotted positions. The steps down into the little valley were steep, irregular and slippery but they all managed to arrive in position within a few minutes. All was silent and the mizzle swirled gently.

Freeman knocked and rang the bell several times. Eventually after what seemed like an eternity it was opened and a woman in a pink dressing gown peered through. It was ironic that the only bit of colour in this dismal setting was from the dressing gown, with the team of armed police dressed in black in stark contrast.

'Yes?' the woman said. She only saw Freeman and Soloman.

'Sonia Upton?'

'Yes,' the reply was slightly hesitant, as if she wasn't sure in what she would be implicating herself.

'We need to speak with you and Mr Brocking, we assume he's in?'

It was a statement and as Freeman said these words he and Soloman moved towards the door and pushed it open, moving the woman back into the hallway, which they then entered.

At the same time there was a commotion at the rear of the cottage as Trevor Brocking tried to make a run for it, out of the back door, whereupon he was apprehended by Jeffers and Hill, who smartly marched him back indoors. The six of them met in the small dark sitting room.

Mr Brocking and Ms Upton were placed on the sofa and Jeffers and Hill stood by the door.

'Off somewhere in a hurry were you?' Freeman began.

Trevor Brocking sat motionless save only for shrugging his shoulders. He looked down at the old and worn-out patterned carpet. He was a man in his mid-forties but he looked considerably younger. He was tall at six foot and of average build but it was obvious that he worked out and was fit. He was wearing a navy blue dressing gown. They had been standing in the equally dismal kitchen making tea, before they had been interrupted.

'We are here about the disappearance of a Mr and Mrs Tamworth. What can you tell us about this?' Freeman said looking directly at them both.

Sonia Upton looked steadfastly and blankly ahead. It was as if she felt she was above answering questions. She managed to look between Freeman and Soloman who were standing directly in front of the sofa.

Trevor Brocking continued to sit motionless and stared between his spread-eagled knees at the worn carpet. From the years of concentrated wear, where countless pairs of feet had been parked the pattern had disappeared.

There was no connection now between the two. That link had been severed. Soloman could see past that and knew that they were deeply involved in the murder and disappearance of the Tamworths.

'We have a warrant to search these premises. I am now arresting you both on the suspicion of the murder of Chris and Bridget Tamworth,' Freeman had spoken again but the suspects on the sofa remained motionless. It was almost as if they had been expecting to be arrested that morning. 'Read them their rights,' Freeman concluded, speaking to Soloman.

He did as he was asked. Trevor Brocking and Sonia Upton were then handcuffed by Jeffers and Soloman and lead away separately to the cars. They were driven away back to Bodmin where they were placed in holding cells.
Soloman and Freeman returned to the cottage to investigate more fully and the armed police section disbanded and drove away.

Chapter 37

DCI Freeman and DC Soloman went upstairs and started searching the two bedrooms. They were not looking for anything in particular, just anything that would be relevant. It was obvious that the first bedroom that they entered was in use. The bed had been slept in and was unmade. It was an old wooden framed item, but not an antique. The wallpaper was old, floral and dirty. In places there were signs of damp and mould. It was peeling in places and together with the sagging and elderly curtains, the room had an unloved feel about it. It was certainly not a desirable place. The original windows were dirty and ill-fitting and a cold damp draught could be felt through them.

In the corner was a wardrobe. One small foot was missing and that corner was propped on a brick. Water marks ran down the front, presumably from a leaking roof above the ceiling. Alongside this was a dressing table with an old mirror. The silvering was now beginning to craze the reflective surface. Apart from an upright chair there was nothing else in this room. Freeman began to examine the contents of the chest of drawers, opening them one by one and giving the underwear inside a quick turn over. Soloman strode over to the wardrobe and flung open the doors. He searched between the hanging jackets, shirts and blouses. Lower down he picked up and looked at the shoes individually. There was nothing unusual or suspicious in these items of clothing.

'It's like the rest of this case,' Freeman said, 'eventually you get a lead, which takes us so far and then there is nothing further. Then another lead sometime later and then nothing again. I rather feel that that is where we are now. There has to be something here.'

The second bedroom was the same. A single grimy bed occupied the space under the window. It had a dirty mattress and was unmade. Apart from a similar upright chair there was no other furniture and bare wooden boards graced the floor. This room was never used.

Freeman and Soloman made their way back down the creaking stairs. A shiver ran down Soloman's spine. He did not feel comfortable in properties such as these.

'I think there may be a couple of rooms off the back hall,' Soloman said, hoping that they might find something by way of compensation for there being nothing upstairs.

The pair made their way through the gloomy hall and living room and into the kitchen.

'What has happened to Greg and Sue?' Freeman asked, 'they were supposed to be with us from the start.

'I'll chase them up,' Soloman said reaching for his phone.

They were now through the kitchen and standing on the broken quarry tiles in the back hall. This part of the building had been built at the same time but was of single storey construction. They stood outside a wooden door. It had rough edges and hadn't been painted or varnished.

'We haven't been in here. I wonder what is through this door.'

He tried the handle but the door did not open. It was securely locked and there was no movement within the door and frame.

'Break the door down,' Freeman urged.

Soloman tried but the door didn't give.

'I'll get the sledgehammer from the car,' Soloman said, rubbing his shoulder.

He returned five minutes later, with the heavy implement.

'Forensics just parking up,' he reported. 'I told them to come straight down.

'Here, give that to me,' Freeman said, holding his hand out for the sledgehammer.

After the second hard strike, the door gave way and swung open. They both looked at each other. They had been expecting at least a creak and a groan but it opened without a shudder or a squeak. The door seemed larger on the inside. It was pitch black as they peered inside and there was a distant hum, the sound perhaps of an air conditioning unit.

Before they had time to go any further, Greg and Sue, from forensics, appeared behind them in the black hall, breathless from carrying equipment down the steep steps outside.

'This is a bit quirky,' Greg said at last.

Freeman and Soloman were more interested with the dark cavern in front of them. Freeman fumbled for where he thought the light switch might be but there was none.

'Try this switch here,' Soloman said, pointing to a switch on the outside of the room in the dark hallway. A bit of a strange place, he thought.

The switch was pressed and the room within was illuminated. They all stepped inside and gasped.

'Don't touch a thing, even with gloves and stay where you are.' Freeman said to Soloman, as the full extent of what lay before them registered in his brain. 'I think we had better let Greg and Sue give this room their full attention, without our interference.'

Soloman stood there, routed to the spot, not quite believing his eyes. The room before him bore no resemblance to the rest of the house. It was like chalk and cheese as though they had stepped through into another world. No expense had been spared on this side of the doorway. The thickly padded door was covered in a black material, making it draught and sound-proof. The room was well illuminated and on closer inspection there was a control panel that gave more lighting options.

The room was a good size, five metres square and the floor was finished in a clean grey rubber covering. On the far side was a low bed, with a silky black padded covering, which draped on all sides to the floor. Matching pillows and cushions in abundance festooned the headboard end.

Beside and opposite the bed, on the door wall were large frameless mirrors. A mid-grey paint had been applied to the walls. It was the large array of objects hanging on special racks and hooks on the two side walls, that Soloman could not take his eyes off.

'Come along now,' Freeman said. 'Is this the first adult playroom that you have seen?'

Soloman was slightly taken aback by the assumption that he might be used to this sort of thing.

'I'm no prude,' he answered, not wishing to appear naive in such matters. 'This sort of thing is all over the internet....' he paused, 'if you wish to look for it, but there is a first time for everything and it just takes a moment to adjust when one sees it in reality.'

He rallied himself and without moving said, 'Well this sums it all up quite succinctly, doesn't it, boss? It looks like Jeffers' theory, at the very beginning, of bondage going one step too far, might be the correct one.'

There was a pause for a moment, while Freeman thought back.

'Yes, you're quite right, he did make that comment didn't he.'

'There's a cupboard over there,' Soloman said, noticing for the first time a flush door, painted in the same grey as the walls. It was barely noticeable.

Greg and Sue stepped forward.

'Shall we start with that then?' They both had their white coveralls on.

'Yes,' Freeman barked, 'good idea.'

The cupboard was locked and there was no sign of a key.

Greg didn't bother to ask and with the crowbar in hand, the door was easily forced, the remains of which swung open to reveal a hanging rail with two items on coat hangers.

There was a gasp from everyone as Sue gently reached inside and lifted down a stylish red leather jacket and a man's Adidas white T-shirt with the three stripes on the shoulders. The items were quickly bagged up and labelled.

'We'll study these first,' Sue said, 'as soon as we get back to the lab. Looks like these are your biggest clues.'

'There doesn't appear to be much more in the rest of the house,' Freeman said, nodding in agreement to Sue's last comment, 'but you may well find something. We haven't been in the loft yet,' he added and turning to Soloman he said, 'we'll leave now and get back to the station. We've seen all we need to here. Greg and Sue will take a proper look, DNA and photographs etc.'

Greg and Sue gave a thumbs up acknowledgement and Freeman and Soloman made their way out of the dismal surroundings and back up the steep and winding steps to the lane above. Soloman was pleased to leave the house. He dreaded to think what may have happened in that sinister hovel with its damp and cracked interior. A shudder went through him as he reached the top step. Freeman was close behind him and feeling the same.

'No,' he said, being sensitive for a change and surprising Soloman, 'I'm just as pleased as you are to leave that ghastly place. We really appreciate what Greg and Sue do for us.'

They both took a few deep breaths as if to cleanse their inner beings.

'We aren't hardened like some forces are,' Freeman summarised.

They walked in silence up the lane. Soloman had a private thought that he had to learn to toughen up in this sort of case, whilst still retaining his sensitive side for when that was more appropriate. He appreciated that it was going to be hard. His sensitive side would always be the stronger, but if he was going to succeed as a sergeant, he had to make some changes.

Their car was parked alone now apart from Greg and Sue's white van, which was some way further down. They had only been two hours, but it felt considerably longer. There was a little more traffic and it was daylight. Their moods did not lift and this was not helped by the descending mist and mizzle.

They travelled in silence and when they reached Bodmin, Freeman spoke, 'I'll lead the questioning, I'm all fired up now and really want to get this case sorted once and for all.'

Chapter 38

Freeman and Soloman climbed wearily out of the car when they arrived back at the police headquarters. It was only just after eight am and they both felt as if they had done a day's work after their early start and the preparations of the night before. It was going to be another long day but they believed that the end was in sight and spurred on by this fact, they set to.

Soloman was desperate to ring Richard for some support. He admitted to himself that he was finding this case hard to deal with. There was so much conflict and there had been such a time span when nothing much had happened. The two persons most badly affected were innocent youngsters, whose lives had been radically changed. They only had each other for support.

As he made his way upstairs to his desk, he found himself thinking that before Richard had come into his life, he would have had to manage on his own. Now he had someone older with more experience of life. He made his way to the coffee machine. Freeman was stood there waiting while his mug filled.

'I'll just be a moment, boss. I need to make a call.'

Freeman gestured that he understand and Soloman made his way onto the roof terrace. The air was still full of mizzle. It was a typical damp grey October morning, though still quite mild. He called Richard's number and waited. He should be in his office suite after his gym session, eating his breakfast and preparing himself for his day.

Eventually his call was answered and a breathless Richard spoke, 'Hi 'O', what's up, how are you doing?' The tone was light and upbeat, at odds with Ore's mood.

'I'm okay, just very tired after an all-nighter and it's not going to end there. It's going to be an all-day kind of day too. It's a bit hard at the moment and I just wanted to hear your voice.'

'I understand,' came back the reply in soft and reassuring tones. 'Anything I can do?'

'No, not really. I just needed to know that you were there for me.'

'You know that I am.'

'Thank you,' Ore replied, 'sorry to have disturbed you. I know that you are busy. I had better go. We are about to have a questioning meeting.'

Richard knew better than to ask for details, 'that is all sounding very positive. I hope that means that you are making progress. I imagine this is to do with the summer case.'

207

'I had better go,' Ore said realising that the others would now be waiting for him.

'Okay, I'll see you soon, yes?'

'Yes, that would be very good.'

'Bye, I love you.'

It was the first time that Richard had used those three little words. There was a pause.

'I love you too,' Ore replied.

The call ended and Ore stood for a moment transfixed by those three words. A warm glow came over him, despite the grey mizzle around him. He hurried back inside.

Chapter 39

Superintendent Louise Marshall was a good police officer. She had diligently worked her way up the police ladder and was now well respected. She was fair with her officers and had the ability to know when a team player was not performing. But she also had a sensitive side and was ready to use it when appropriate. These qualities applied to her colleagues and team members and also in some respects to those who needed to be brought to justice. Police work is not only confined to criminals. There are those in the community that the force comes into daily contact that need help and a more sensitive approach.

Superintendent Marshall called an impromptu meeting that morning. Now that the two persons had been brought in, she very much wanted to be a part of the proceedings and not just be brought up to date after the event.

Dressed in her usual office wear of a smart black jacket and trousers, with a white blouse, she made a striking figure. At five foot eleven and of slim build she only ever wore flat shoes. Discreet makeup added to this sensible approach.

Freeman led the team into the meeting room where Superintendent Marshall was already seated and smiling. They all sat down with their cups of coffee in hand. Most had managed to grab a snack beforehand. It had already been a long morning.

Still smiling, Marshall began. 'Good morning everyone and well done with all your achievements, an excellent result. Your planning and diligence has paid off.'

A note of agreement went around the room. This was praise indeed and they were all grateful for the acknowledgement of their hard work.

'DCI Freeman will now bring us fully up to date. Perhaps you could start with anything that the forensics team have found out since you arrived back here.'

Everyone turned towards Freeman. He rose and faced his audience. 'Communication by mobile with Greg and Sue has been futile. The property, as we all know, is down in a deep ravine. We are now speaking on the landline and they are continuing their search. Two items of special interest to us were found in a locked cupboard in the adult playroom,' Freeman paused and looked firstly at Marshall and then around the room.

'You had better clarify exactly what you mean,' Marshall said immediately.

Freeman was a true professional and without a hint of embarrassment described quite graphically the room behind the soundproofed door. He explained how it was a complete opposite to the rest of the house, both in its nature and also in the amount of money that had been lavished on it.

The team scribbled and tapped frantically. They were used to extreme issues in cases and took it all in their stride.

'It seems, Jeffers,' Freeman said turning directly to him, 'that you were probably correct in your assumptions all those months ago. It is likely that we are dealing with a bondage situation that either got

210

out of control or was intentional by the two persons that we are holding downstairs. Either way, they are guilty, as they should have reported the incident. So far we have seen no remorse and indeed Mr Brocking did try to escape through the back door when we arrived. We found a red leather jacket and a man's white sports T-shirt in the cupboard which we had to break open. These appear to be "trophy items", as there doesn't appear to be any evidence at present that the Tamworth's have ever been in the house. Greg and Sue will continue there as long as is necessary. We will be interviewing the suspects separately after this meeting.'

'Just to be clear,' Marshall began again, 'the trophy items have yet to be tested for DNA etc and it appears that there is nothing else that ties Mr Brocking and Ms Upton to the deceased couple at the cottage.'

'Yes, that is correct but we know that the Tamworths were travelling in Mr Brocking's car around the time that they went missing. The ligature marks on their wrists and ankles do rather connect them with that room. Mr Brocking's car had a puncture repaired at Jago's Garage in Liskeard at the end of June.' He stopped. 'How stupid am I? We've forgotten about the little red Fiat,' Freeman turned to Soloman, 'get that car collected and brought back here. Forensics will need to give that a thorough inspection too. With the discovery of the room I had completely forgotten about the car.'

'Consider it done boss,' Soloman said. 'I had forgotten about it too.'

'Well that sums up our findings so far and brings everyone up to date, we'll start our questioning now.'

The meeting was terminated and Superintendent Marshall looked pleased   with   the   progress.

Chapter 40

'We'll question him first,' Freeman said to Soloman. 'Get him brought up to Room One, it's empty I believe.'

Trevor Brocking's brief had been waiting patiently and together they all assembled in the interview room. Mr Brocking was brought from his cell.

He was now dressed in a grey sweatpants and shirt. He looked unkempt and tired but also indifferent to his current situation.

After the formalities had been conducted and introductions made, Freeman started. 'You are here in connection with the disappearance of Mr and Mrs Tamworth. They haven't been seen since last June. What can you tell us about your involvement in this matter?'

There was no eye contact from Trevor Brocking. His head was bowed and his shoulders stooped. However, he did not have the aggressive appearance of someone capable of such a murder. Freeman had been here before and knew only too well that looks could be very deceptive. Certainly, the figure in front of him was a broken man. Eventually after more coaxing, a rather quiet 'no comment' was uttered.

Freeman tried again on a slightly different tack. 'We have you and Ms Upton on CCTV at a garage in Liskeard with Mr and Mrs Tamworth, when you had a tyre repaired. We know that you were with them. Tell us about that afternoon?'

There was no response from the slumped figure but a whispered word from his brief seemed to rouse him momentarily.

Mr Brocking opened his mouth to speak and there was a flash from a prominent gold tooth. He sat up straight and looked completely different. Now one could imagine a different character, Soloman thought.

Finally, he spoke. 'We had a slow puncture and finally that afternoon we had it repaired. We have a small car and with four on board, it seemed to lose air much more quickly. I don't know anything else about those people you mention.'

Without missing a beat, Freeman spoke again. 'Tell us about the red leather jacket and the sports shirt found in the locked wardrobe in your special room in the cottage.'

It was an order but Brocking slumped and fell silent again.

In the next room, through the mirrored glass, the others looked on expectantly. Sometimes it was good to jump around with lots of different questions fired one after another. The result was to slightly unnerve the recipient to try to achieve any answer, which might ultimately lead to another.

Downstairs in her cell, Sonia Upton lay on her back on the cold hard concrete bench, gazing up and not particularly thinking about anything.

Having nudged his client, the brief lent forwards and again whispered in Brocking's ear. It seemed to take an age for this information to sink in before Brocking replied, with the now customary and unhelpful, 'no comment!'

Those on the other side of the mirror were slightly taken aback when Freeman abruptly stood up and announced, 'Interview terminated at 14.24 hours.'

He walked towards the door, speaking as he strode, 'Take him back to his cell.'

He left the room and walked over to the coffee machine at the end of the corridor. Brocking was led away in the opposite direction back to his cell.

'So, what's your plan?' Freeman heard a voice behind him.

It was Soloman who joined him at the drinks machine.

'He only agreed that they had all been together in the car that afternoon when the slow puncture was being fixed.' Soloman said, placing his mug and pressing the relevant buttons, for a strong black coffee.

They made their way through a glass door marked 'Fire Exit' and walked onto a wide metal walkway outside. They were overlooking a few cars and a hedge that bounded a wheat field. It was a good quiet place to contemplate the current case, after the austerity of an interview room. The latter was of course air conditioned like the rest of the building but it was certainly good to feel and breathe some fresh air. Sometimes this walkway was the place that private conversations were held, sometimes sensitive issues. It was also a kind of unofficial sanctuary, known to all. Everyone seemed to go there, when a little respite was needed and that was why Freeman and Soloman had made their way there now. They gazed out in silence over the wheat field, taking in the air and peaceful surroundings.

How could such terrible things happen? Soloman thought to himself.

His thinking was interrupted by Freeman. 'I want to talk to Ms Upton next. See if I can get more out of her than Brocking. I want to let him have a little time to think about our questions and then we will get back to him.'

A few moments later, Freeman made to move and Soloman dutifully followed. They returned to the interview room and Sonia Upton was brought from her cell. Her brief joined them and they all sat down.

The introductions were made and Freeman started again with the same questions. 'We have seen you and Trevor, on CCTV, at the garage in Liskeard with Mr and Mrs Tamworth having a tyre repaired on your car, a small red Fiat, at the end of June. What happened next after you left?'

Sonia Upton was a tall slim woman in her late thirties. She had short dark hair, cut stylishly. She had pleasant if not rather severe features and in any other circumstances, she would have passed for a smart capable executive. She was now dressed in a red T-shirt and black sweatpants with no makeup and unwashed, slightly greasy hair.

She sat upright in her chair unlike Brocking and stared rather unnervingly at Freeman, almost through him. Freeman sat waiting for her answer.

'We went for a drink.'

'Where?' Freeman quickly responded.

'I don't know, some bar in Looe.'

'After that?' Freeman hurried on as if he felt that Upton was on a roll answering questions.

'We went back to the cottage.'

'To Treworthy Cottage, in Looe?'

Sonia Upton fell silent. Were they getting closer to the truth?

'We know you stayed there at this exact time,' Freeman said. 'You gave Treworthy Cottage as the address to Jago Motors and we have your details confirmed as renting the cottage for this period, by Sea Breeze Holiday Homes.'

After such a good start, Freeman and Soloman were disappointed with the answer.

'No comment.'

It was as if Sonia Upton was drip-feeding information to them at her own pace. In her mind she was almost leading the proceedings.

Freeman repeated the question but all Sonia said in answer was, 'yes we rented that cottage, you know that, why ask what you already know?'

Freeman let it go and proceeded with, 'in your special room, in your cottage, how do you explain the red jacket and man's T-shirt in the locked wardrobe?'

Without a moment's hesitation or flicker, Sonia said, 'Mr and Mrs Tamworth gave them to us.'

'Seems a little odd,' Soloman said quickly, realising that he hadn't said a word. 'Why would one couple give another couple two garments, one particularly special? It was an anniversary present.'

Sonia Upton just shrugged her shoulders in recognition of the question but that was all Freeman or Soloman could get out of her.

After a further fifteen minutes of unanswered questions, Freeman terminated the interview and again he and Soloman found themselves at the coffee machine.

Shortly afterwards they returned back to the viewing room next door and on Freeman's instructions, Trevor Brocking was brought in. They peered back through the viewing glass.

'I wanted to see how he was now before I went back in there, now he has had time to think about my questions. He will be wondering how we got on with Sonia.'

Superintendent Louise Marshall sat motionless in the room. She had seen it all before but she trusted Freeman and his methods.

'Keep at it,' she said. 'You'll soon crack them. We just need a confession, preferably from them both.' She smiled briefly.

Trevor Brocking looked a broken man, far worse than when they had seen him forty minutes before. His hair was even more dishevelled, his face grey and his eyes were greatly sunken. As Freeman and Soloman re-entered the room he did not raise his head.

Freeman started the proceedings. 'The red leather jacket and T-shirt in the wardrobe, you kept those as trophies didn't you, having strangled Mr and Mrs Tamworth?'
Trevor Brocking looked at his brief and then very quietly said, 'I can't deny it. We did keep the items. I really don't know why. We should have ditched them, along with the bodies.'

There was a pause in the room and a sharp intake of breath in the room next door, from those watching. Was this an admission? At this point Trevor Brocking realised what he had said.

'I can't bear it!' he quietly mumbled

'Again, for the tape please, a little louder,' Soloman gently encouraged.

It was repeated and it seemed as if a switch had been turned. Communication was now happening.

It all started out as just some fun and I never meant it to go all the way, they just wanted to try this near-death, asphyxiation technique. I blame Sonia! She's always had a cruel streak and now this has happened. Once they were dead we just had to get rid of the bodies and she seemed to have it all worked out. I have never known her like that before. She even knew where to bury them and what to do with the car. She must have planned it all and just used me as an accomplice to further her dark needs. I saw a different side to her and whilst I had always been happy to partake in the legal side, I certainly never wanted to do what happened to them. It was her idea to keep the jacket and the T-shirt.'

He paused as if waiting for recognition of what he had just imported. He needed to know if what he was saying was what the police officers wanted to hear.

'Explain to us exactly what happened to the Tamworths in Treworthy Cottage?'

Trevor Brocking recalled how Chris and Bridget had been complicit in going to the cottage and for swapping partners. They had also agreed to being tied up and to try the auto-asphyxiation experience. They had agreed the use of "safe words" but at the last moment these had been ignored.

'In summary,' Freeman started, 'you admit to murdering Bridget Tamworth, whilst Ms Upton murdered Chris Tamworth, at the same time, in the next room?'

'I suppose when you put it like that, that is what happened.'

'In that case,' Freeman said, 'Soloman, charge him with the murder of Bridget Tamworth and with complicity in the murder of Chris Tamworth.'

Five minutes later, he was taken back to his cell and Freeman and Soloman joined the others in the adjoining room for a debriefing.

218

'I knew we would get there in the end,' Sheila said. There was relief in her voice.

Around the room, everyone agreed, several hi fives were exchanged and smiles reappeared.

'Yes, any progress is good, however Upton is the harder nut to crack. We aren't there quite yet.' Marshall said bringing everyone back to reality. 'One to go, I'll leave you with it. I've a meeting in five minutes, let me know how you get on.'

Jeffers was dispatched to the canteen for sandwiches, so that they could have a working, if rather late, lunch.

Forty five minutes later, Freeman and Soloman were back in the interview room. Sonia Upton had been brought back up and her general demeanour had been noted through the viewing glass. This time, she also looked a little less confident but the cockiness was still evident.

Freeman began. 'We know exactly what happened at Treworthy Cottage, after a full and frank confession from Mr Brocking, so there is no point in denying any of it. It will certainly help your case if you now admit what you have done.'

After a minute and a consultation with her brief, she replied, 'No comment!'

Ms Upton looked at her brief after there was no reaction from either Freeman or Soloman and indeed, both had sat back in their chairs and looked past Ms Hill.

Finally, after about five minutes of silence, Sonia Hill gave up and admitted that she was responsible for the murder of Chris Tamworth. She did not however admit to leading the events of that afternoon and would not admit to suggesting how or where to place the bodies or what to do with the car.

Rather surprisingly she had admitted that both she and Brocking had removed the bodies in their own clothes, minus the red jacket and T-shirt, placed them in the Auris which she had driven to the bottom of Harry Winds' field. They had stumbled across this by accident, whilst driving from Looe in the early hours. Brocking had followed in their car, the red Fiat. It had seemed to him that Upton had planned the burial spot. Together they dug the graves in the leaf mould and then set fire to the car, having pushed it over the edge. There had been no exploding fuel tank or any noise from the fire, which was contained in the pit, the fuel tank being practically empty. The car had completely burnt out and no one had been any the wiser. By the time the first car had driven along the lane, a few hours later, the car was no more than a smouldering wreck, well hidden from view. Even Harry Winds, in his early morning drunken haze had seen a small plume of smoke, from the breakfast table but put it down to a neighbouring farm across the lane. His wife had not dared to question this.

When questioned later, Trevor Brocking had described how he had been carried along with the situation. After this, they had driven back to The Old Smithy, in Liskeard and cleared it of the Tamworth's belongings. They had just finished in time, before the street became busy and to anyone passing, they appeared as a pair of holiday makers leaving early. They had left, leaving the key in the keysafe and a thank you note on the hall table to the owners, complementing them on their lovely cottage.

They had returned to Treworthy Cottage, where they had cleared up, packed and left later that morning, returning to their own home by lunchtime. A bonfire had taken place in the garden and all the Tamworth's belongings had been systematically burnt.

Sonia Upton was charged with the murder of Chris Tamworth and complicity in the murder of his wife. She too was taken back to her cell.

Later that evening, Freeman received a message from the forensic team stating that after the red Fiat had been checked, the

Tamworth's DNA had been found in the form of hairs from Mrs Tamworth and a used tissue from Mr Tamworth, the later having been pushed down the back of the rear seat.

Chapter 41

Later that day, Freeman telephoned Willoughby and Oliver-Jones. He gave them a full account of the arrest and they then made their way to the Tamworth's home. Karen the receptionist at the Leisure Centre was informed also and appeared almost immediately. She had long ago decided that when the inevitable news came, she would be there for Simon and Vanessa. She ended up moving into the spare bedroom for two weeks.

Media coverage was intense, across all networks and Simon and Vanessa spent most of that week sheltering indoors. Karen used her people skills, gleaned from dealing with the general public to fend off the press and media at the front door. Gradually the interest lessened, only to rise up again when the case went to court, one month later.

The inhabitants of Looe, Liskeard and Tintagel were horrified, that such a vicious and horrific crime had been committed in their own peaceful Cornwall.

'Such things really don't happen here.' Doris Silvers was heard to say, in the post office the next day. She gave a good impression of being deeply affected by it all, especially as she had stood so close to the actual murderers and their victims. Secretly she loved all the attention that she was receiving and when a reporter knocked on her front door, asking for an interview, he had never received such a warm welcome. Doris served him tea from her best tea service and the young man from The Cornish Times had difficulty leaving.

Nigel and Susan Rathbone, the owners of Treworthy Cottage were very relieved that it was all over but within a month, as the end of the year approached, more visitors seemed to be arriving in Harbour Street and gathered round the now infamous front door. Some of these found their way up the street and into the art gallery.

Trevor Brocking and Sonia Upton were both given life sentences. In the judge's summary, she made it quite clear, that she and the rest of the court had been horrified and that there was no room in today's society, or any other, for these kind of abominations.

Chapter 42

Freeman and Soloman, not to mention the rest of the team, were exhausted, by the end of the two confessions.

Soon after this had been filed, they and their colleagues left for their own homes. It had been a gruelling few days, physically and mentally.

As Soloman drove, he appreciated that Cornwall was not the sleepy place that his former colleagues from Reading had jokingly intimated at the time of his moving from one force to another. This was his second high-profile case and he wondered if he would receive any communications from his former colleagues, now that his name and face were beginning to appear on the news.

It was a beautiful evening but he was so tired that he knew that he would struggle to keep awake. As he reached his flat, he knew what he must do first. He opened the French doors onto his balcony, sat down and called Richard. It was only to be a short call.

Richard was very pleased to hear from him. Their last communication had been brief just before the interviews.

'Yes, it's all finished now bar the court case. Thank goodness for those confessions and now the boss has given me the day off tomorrow, so I expect I will just sleep,' he concluded, 'so I'll say nighty-nite and I'll ring again tomorrow to arrange a meet up when I feel less tired.'

Half an hour later, Ore fell asleep and slept soundly for the next twelve hours.

He awoke to a bright sunny morning. He could tell that rain had fallen overnight, from the wetness on the roof window above his head. He gazed up at the bright sunshine which was now lower in the blue sky and the white clouds that were passing overhead.

He swung his legs out of bed feeling very much refreshed and having made some breakfast he was sitting contemplating a quiet day catching up at home. He must call his mother whom he had not spoken to for more than a week. At that moment, his doorbell rang.

Strange, he thought, someone's passed the main door and is now outside his.

Upon opening the door, there stood a beaming Richard.

'Should've phoned, I know, but I have some big news to tell you, which I have to do in person. At the same time, I am rather anxious as I never discussed this with you and I am not sure how you will feel.'

Richard paused waiting for a reaction. Ore who was just recovering from the surprise of seeing Richard, wasn't quite sure what to think and cautiously said, 'Go on.'

'I've got a new job,' he excitedly said, 'at The Cove Hotel.'

There was another pause, while Ore absorbed this double piece of news.

'You know, where I took you, it's a promotion, it's one of our flagship exclusive Spa Hotels. The guest list is very impressive. It has been successfully promoted across Europe. I shall be dealing with top celebrities and the rich and famous. It is going to be very demanding and my team is going to have to be the very best.'

'I'm really pleased for you, well done. That is such good news,' Ore paused, 'why should I mind?'

I'm just checking that you are happy with the fact that I shall be moving down to Cornwall.'

Appendix

And what happened to Simon and Vanessa Tamworth, I hear you ask?'

As one would imagine, life was a struggle for them both as it would be for anyone losing their parents in such horrific circumstances. The timings of these occurrences in their lives was devastating, being so young and with no family members there to support them. Karen became a second mum to them both.

They both tried to cope with all the unanswered questions that were inevitable. What were Mum and Dad thinking of getting involved with such people? Why did it have to happen to them? Why did we know nothing about this part of their lives and why did they have to leave us just now when everything was going so well and we had only recently moved into our new home?

Floods of differing emotions filled each day, anger, hate, desperation, helplessness and even self-loathing.

The school student welfare officer at Vanessa's school spent many long hours with her and became a close friend. It was a difficult time for them both. After an initial period of complete despair lasting several months Vanessa rallied and went on to do reasonably well in her A level exams.

Simon went to University in Chichester and despite all odds did well in his course receiving a high pass in Sports and Leisure management. He continued to work at the swimming baths as a lifeguard during his studies. Dave gave him greater responsibilities as his course proceeded and acted as a mentor to him.

Simon and Vanessa decided to continue living in the new family home on the estate but they never felt either settled or comfortable. By the time that Vanessa had passed through university and been successful in achieving a job in publishing in London, both decided that it was time to sell up and forge their own paths.

By this time, Simon had a girlfriend and a baby son. With his half of the proceeds of the family home, he and Janine bought a new three bedroomed house in the last phase of building on that particular estate. He was at last settled and happy with his new family. Auntie Vanessa travelled down from London once a month to see her nephew and they remained as close as they ever had been.

Printed in Great Britain
by Amazon